A CHRISTMAS CONSPIRACY

Painting conservator Grace is excited to be joining the Christmas celebrations at a rural French château, along with her dress-designer sister Natasha. She's looking forward to helping her sister put on a fashion show, studying the château's extensive collection of paintings, taking part in a murder mystery evening — and perhaps falling in love with her hostess's son, bad-boy singer-songwriter Kai Curtis. But events soon start to take a sinister turn . . .

KATE FINNEMORE

A CHRISTMAS CONSPIRACY

Complete and Unabridged

LINFORD
Leicester

First published in Great Britain in 2018

First Linford Edition
published 2022

*A catalogue record for this book is available
from the British Library.*

ISBN 978–1–4448–4977–6

Published by
Ulverscroft Limited
Anstey, Leicestershire

Printed and bound in Great Britain by
TJ Books Ltd., Padstow, Cornwall

This book is printed on acid-free paper

Love-Struck

'Wow,' Grace breathed, as she caught tantalising glimpses between the trees of the Château Beauvallon, their destination for the week ahead.

She didn't like to voice her excitement, in case she distracted her sister Natasha who sat hunched over the steering wheel, driving in second gear along the narrow country lane.

The motorways and main roads had been cleared of snow, but here it lay on the ground still, compacted and glistening, as treacherous as an ice-rink. The snow-filled ditches on each side were an additional potential hazard.

Natasha darted her sister the briefest of looks.

'Not far now, thank goodness.'

So she, too, had glimpsed the château.

'Just in time for mid-morning coffee,' Grace said. She saw her sister glance down at the phone that lay between them by the handbrake. The sat nav app was

1

running. 'Keep your eyes on the road, Nat,' she warned gently.

She looked out again at the winter-white forest that stretched away on both sides. A thick dusting of frost covered the dark trunks and leafless branches that stood motionless in the still air as if frozen.

Beyond the trees on her left, she could see the creamy white walls of the château, a tower with battlements at its top, pointed Gothic windows and gently arching Romanesque ones.

Delight brought a smile to her face. The architecture was haphazard, quirky, a wonderful mish-mash of styles. She was going to enjoy it here, she thought.

And that was when it happened. Natasha's phone pinged. For a split second, they both looked down at it. The car tyres lost traction and the car skidded — oh, so slowly — over the icy surface.

In an instant, Grace reached across to the steering wheel to turn the vehicle into the skid. It helped, but not enough. The car glided a few metres more before the driver's side rear wheel slid down into the ditch.

For a long moment, the two sisters could only sit there. Grace's heart was beating an uneasy rhythm. Her sister's, too, she guessed, judging by the look of shock in her eyes. The car was at an angle, sloping downwards to the ditch.

'The perfect way,' Natasha said with heavy irony, 'to start our Christmas break.'

'At least we're not hurt.' Reaching behind her, Grace took the two hi-viz vests from under the pile of clothes, each garment protected by polythene, laid out on the back seat.

There were more in the boot, Grace knew, carefully wrapped in tissue paper and stored in boxes. She handed one of the vests to her sister.

'Put this on,' she said, pulling her own on over her padded jacket.

'Good old Grace,' Natasha said with a laugh. 'As practical as ever.'

Grace laughed, too, relieved that the look of shock had left her sister's face.

'One of us has to be. Stay here a moment. I'll see how close to the edge you are.' It was strange pushing up against the weight of the car door to open it and when she did, icy air hit her face.

She scrambled outside, letting the door slam shut behind her, and made her way gingerly round the front of the car, glad she was wearing sensible fleece-lined boots with ridged soles. She reached the driver's side, and the breath stopped in her throat.

Three of the four wheels were safely on the ground. But the fourth hung as if suspended in empty space. Any hope she might have had of stuffing grass and twigs under it to give it purchase before driving off again vanished on the spot. They'd have to call out a breakdown truck. And with their limited French that wouldn't be easy.

At her nod, Natasha opened the driver's side door and eased herself out. She stood on the narrowing wedge of ground between the front of the car and the ditch, puffing out a breath as she looked

4

at the rear wheel.

'Your French is better than mine,' she said. 'How about you phone a garage and get them to send someone out? I'll call the breakdown insurance guys.'

'I'd better put the warning triangle out first,' Grace said, edging back round the front of the car.

'Take care, Gracie.'

'You, too.'

Grace took the light plastic triangle out of the boot and carried it back the way they'd come. She walked on the grass verge between the road and the ditch where the snow was fluffy still, and not at all slippery, counting her paces. The triangle had to be about 30 metres, or 60 steps, away from the car.

Taking her phone out of her jeans pocket as she hurried along, she started to look for the nearest garage. She could hear a car approaching, saw it in the distance coming towards her, and broke into a jog.

The driver had seen her. He slowed, coming to a halt a metre or so from where she'd set the warning triangle down. The car's dove grey paintwork had been dulled by the ice and snow that had splashed up from the road. Even so, it was an impressive vehicle, a low sleek sports car with smoked glass windows and an engine that growled.

The engine fell silent. Grace watched, a polite smile on her face, as the car door opened and its occupant got out.

But I know that face, she thought. I know this man. A jolt of recognition sped through her, puzzlement too for the barest fraction of a second. And then she placed him, and her heart swept into a crazy pitter-patter. No, not a personal acquaintance, but someone known to countless millions of music fans in the UK. In Europe too. And in the US of course.

Her gaze went from his dark hair to those arching eyebrows over beautiful eyes, to the strong line of his jaw, to the long leather coat he wore — and all at once it was as if ten years had been lopped off her age and she was a love-struck, hero-worshipping teenager rather than a mature young woman.

Singer-songwriter sensation Kai Curtis was coming towards her, moving with easy long-legged grace. In moments, she'd be within touching distance. He'd say something to her, he was bound to. And she'd say something back. Just him and her, talking together. She'd be the envy of all her friends.

She smiled, more a smile to herself than a greeting to the new arrival. She was being ridiculous, she had to pull herself together.

'Thank you for stopping, Mr — uh — Curtis,' she said, pleased that she sounded her usual sensible self.

His answering smile was brief and meaningless.

'It's the law. I had no choice.'

She blinked, taken aback. His words had been curt to the point of rudeness.

'Oh,' she said stiffly.

He looked beyond her to her sister's car.

'You skidded?'

'Yes.' Grace, too, looked. Natasha had come round the car and was leaning against the passenger-side door, phone to her ear. She was 'wearing the product' as she put it, and looked stunning, as always, today in a full-length coat of palest blue with a matching Dr Zhivago-style hat.

'Who's that? A friend?'

'My sister.' She too could be monosyllabic, she thought grimly, aware she was reacting badly to the admiration she'd heard in his voice. There were purplish smudges beneath his eyes, she saw with some concern, and he hadn't shaved that morning. Had he been driving all night, she wondered, in these difficult conditions?

'Are you both OK?' he asked.

'Yes, thanks, we're fine. But I need to phone for a breakdown truck to get the car out of the ditch.'

'No need,' he surprised her by saying. He reached into his coat pocket and fetched out a phone. 'I'll get one of the neighbours to bring his tractor out.'

'One of the neighbours?'

Something like irritation flashed into his eyes.

'Forget I said that.' Turning partly away, he opened his phone and was soon speaking into it in fluent French.

Of course he was annoyed, she thought, hugging her arms across her chest and stamping up and down on the spot to stop the cold seeping into her bones. Annoyed with himself. He'd let slip information that he was no doubt usually careful to keep private.

Kai Curtis snapped his phone shut.

'Jérôme will be here in a few minutes. So let's get over to your car. Hop in.'

He gestured to his own car and stayed close to her as she made her way round to the passenger side — to catch her if she slipped?

He was an odd mix, she decided. His attitude was just — only just — the right side of rudeness, a vivid contrast to the thoughtfulness he'd also revealed.

He opened the door for her. As she got in, she glimpsed a guitar in its case

9

on the back seat behind her. Kai Curtis's famous 12-string guitar, she thought, and her pulses leaped as she recalled his latest hit, a powerful haunting lament to a lost love.

Moments later, Kai was sitting in the driver's seat. But he didn't start the car straight away.

'You know who I am,' he said, turning to look at her. 'But please don't ask me for a selfie. Or an autograph.'

Grace frowned, noting the tiredness in that famous voice and the pallor of his face. It was warm in the car, and the scent of leather upholstery and the smoky notes of his aftershave filled the air.

'I wasn't going to. Though my sister might. She's been to quite a few of your concerts.'

'My concerts.' The look on his face was bleak. 'Yeah.' Abruptly he turned to face forward, turned the key and brought the engine to growling life.

He drove with confidence, she noted, as he came to a smooth halt a metre or so behind Grace and Natasha's car.

'I got through to the breakdown . . .' Natasha stopped in mid-sentence, eyes widening as she saw who was getting out of the driver's side of the sports car.

'Mr Curtis lives round here. He's arranged for someone to come with their tractor to get us out of the ditch.' Quickly Grace filled her sister in on what was happening.

Turning to Kai, Natasha beamed him a smile.

'You live round here? You're a neighbour of Angela's? Wow, she never said.'

'You know Angela?'

'Angela Beauvallon de Mottefort. Yes. She owns the château over there,' Natasha said, pointing. 'She's invited Grace and me to stay for Christmas.'

'You're guests of Angela's?'

Only one word could describe the look on his face, Grace thought. Appalled. And it wasn't the cold that sent a shiver of unease down her spine. There was something here she didn't understand.

She heard him swear under his breath,

11

and he turned away, pushing his fingers through his hair in a gesture that spoke of immense weariness.

'That's all I need,' he muttered.

Close to You

A rook cawed high in the trees, loud in the silence. The occasional snowflake drifted downwards, soundlessly, and Grace looked up at the blanket of white cloud covering the sky. It was going to snow again.

Putting his phone to his ear, Kai Curtis headed a few metres down the road.

Grace looked at her sister.

'I can't believe it,' she whispered. 'Kai Curtis.'

Glancing up from the screen of her phone, Natasha rolled her eyes.

'Thanks for the info, ' she whispered back. 'I'd never have recognised him.'

Grace felt herself flush.

'You're not wearing the hi-vis vest,' she retorted.

'Neither is Kai.'

Grace looked across at him. He was speaking low into the phone. She couldn't hear what he was saying, but his tone and the movements of his free hand were unmistakably angry.

'No surprise there,' she said. 'He's built his reputation on breaking every rule in the book.'

Standing beside her sister, she watched in silence as he swung round, flipping his phone shut, and made his way back to them.

A flurry of wind brought a swirl of snowflakes with it, but that didn't explain the shiver that sped down her spine as he came to a halt less than a metre from her. His expression was grim.

'I've just been on the phone to my mother. It seems she's invited you to the château for the Christmas . . .'

'Your mother?' Grace cut in. 'Angela is your mother?'

A curt nod.

'One of you is a dress designer. You, I imagine,' he said to Natasha.

'That's right,' she acknowledged with a smile.

'You've come a day ahead of the others,' he stated, 'to get things ready for a fashion show.'

14

'Right again.'

Grace saw him close his eyes for a brief second, and it was another glimpse of the tiredness she'd seen earlier. No, not tiredness — weariness, a bone-weariness that went well beyond mere tiredness.

'Look,' she said, 'we don't want to be a nuisance. We don't have to stay at the château. We can find a B and B somewhere.

We don't have to do a fashion show even.'

Natasha shot her a look.

'Hey . . .'

Kai shook his head.

'It's my mother's house. She's free to invite whoever she wants. Plus it's started snowing again. I couldn't in all conscience send you away.'

He drew in a long breath, looking in the direction Grace and Natasha had been travelling as the low rumble of something large and heavy coming towards them made itself heard.

'If anyone goes, it'll be me,' he went on, watching the tractor as it stopped a short distance away. 'But the place is big enough for all of us. We should be able to keep out of each other's way.'

Grace pulled a laughing face at her sister, the antagonism of a few moments before forgotten. For sheer ungraciousness, his last words surely took the prize.

Jérôme, the tractor driver, jumped down from his vehicle. It was clear the two men knew each other well. With much laughter, he pulled Kai into a hug before coming over to shake hands with Grace and Natasha.

Getting back into his tractor, he turned it round and reversed up to Natasha's car. In no time at all, he and Kai had unreeled the cable from the back of the tractor, attached it to fixing points and pulled the car out of the ditch.

'Wow, they've made it look so easy,' Natasha said.

'Merci. Merci beaucoup,' Grace said, dredging up her schoolgirl French as Jérôme wrapped her hands in both his for another handshake. 'Kai, could you thank him for us, please? We're so grateful. Grateful and relieved.'

There followed an exchange in rapid French between the two men and more laughter before Jérôme clapped Kai on the back and walked back to his tractor. The snow was falling faster now, settling on the vehicles and on everyone's clothes.

'It's not far to the château, a couple of hundred metres, but will you be all right?' Kai asked, touching his hand to Natasha's sleeve.

There it was, Grace thought, that touch, a fraction longer than was necessary. Emotion tugged inside her.

Natasha smiled.

'We'll be fine.'

'I'll be following, if anything happens. Get back in the car now and wait for me. I'm going to fetch your warning triangle.'

The two sisters sat in the car in silence. Natasha was looking at the screen of her phone while Grace kept her eyes on the wing mirror, following Kai's progress back up the road.

The direction her thoughts had taken disturbed her. Natasha was stunning to look at. It was only natural that people admired her. Normally, Grace took it in her stride. She didn't mind. So why did she now react with — what? envy? jealousy? — at the way Kai Curtis's hand had lingered on her sister's sleeve?

★ ★ ★

The small convoy set off, the tractor in front, followed by Natasha driving once again with fierce concentration, with Kai in his sports car bringing up the rear.

Grace sat taut and alert, willing her sister on. They were travelling through a monochrome world, the dark trunks and branches of the trees, all straight lines and sharp angles, veiled by the gently falling snowflakes. So beautiful — but dangerous, too.

The lane grew narrower still as it veered sharply to the left. A short while later, to Grace's relief, they came to the gatehouse that marked the entrance to the Château Beauvallon.

Jérôme and his tractor left them at that point, continuing on while Natasha and Grace, and Kai behind them, turned into the drive, the trees that lined each side marking the way.

Natasha slowed as they reached the turning circle in front of the château. Its façade rose before them, tall and imposing. Two flights of stairs in an elongated S-shape, one the mirror image of the other, curved up to the ornately carved entrance doors. At one corner stood a circular tower that was almost as high as the ridge of the château roof.

'What a fabulous place,' Grace breathed.

Kai eased his car past theirs, indicating they should follow him round to the other side of the château, the side they hadn't seen from the road. The high double doors of one of the outbuildings stood open, and Natasha followed Kai inside.

'Well done,' Grace said when Natasha finally turned the car engine off.

Natasha puffed out a breath and laughed, visibly relaxing.

'I'm glad that's over.'

They were in a vast high space, Grace saw, getting out. It must once have been a barn. Now it housed cars — four, including theirs, with room for two or three more.

At the far end were several curi-ous-looking tractors, perched too high, surely, on their axles. Something to do with winemaking, perhaps. The Château Beauvallon was famous for its wines.

Kai was pushing one of the tall wooden doors shut, and Grace crossed swiftly to do the same to the other one.

'Someone keeps the hinges well-oiled,' she said with a smile as the two doors met in the middle. Snowflakes, blown in from outside, had landed on Kai's hair, and she had to resist the urge to brush them away.

'My stepfather,' he said. 'You can't fault his efficiency.'

A strange turn of phrase? Grace wondered, implying as it did that something else could be faulted. Or was it Kai's tiredness speaking? The purplish smudges under his eyes were more pronounced than ever.

'My mother's waiting in the kitchen,' he went on. 'I'll take you through to her.'

'I'm looking forward to it. I've never met her, but Natasha's told me lots about her.'

He glanced behind him.

'She and your sister have a lot in common.'

Grace too looked across to where Natasha, tall and slender, superbly graceful in the coat and hat she'd designed and made herself, leaned back against the car, head bent as she looked down at the phone in her hand.

Again, Grace felt that twist of emotion — envy? — deep inside her.

'Well, that's good,' she murmured, looking away.

They didn't need to go back out into the snow. She and Natasha each took their suitcase out of the boot — they'd come back later for the clothes for the fashion show — and, with all three wheeling their cases behind them, they followed Kai to a door at the rear of the barn which led to an enclosed walkway.

'Purpose-built,' he said, and about 30 metres and two 90-degree turns further on, he spoke again. 'Here we are. Mind your heads.'

It was a low, wide, dark oak door studded with nails. Hanging from it was a bright, welcoming Christmas wreath, sprigs of pine needles, glossy green holly leaves and ruby red berries, tied with a red and green tartan bow.

Standing back to let the two sisters go first, Kai stretched out his arm to push the door open.

Grace stood with Natasha by her side on the threshold of the kitchen. Warmth billowed out, enveloping her, and with it the fragrant scents of coffee percolating and sweet pastries fresh from the oven.

She took in the large room with its high ceiling crossed by smoke-blackened beams, the walls of natural stone, the long table that filled the centre of the room, the bowls of fruit and candles in silver candlesticks.

But what caught and held her attention was the woman who stood by the fireplace on the opposite side of the room. Tall and striking in silk pyjamas that Grace recognised as one of her sister's designs, she had her face in profile as she gazed up at something on her left.

Grace smiled to herself. Angela Beauvallon de Mottefort must have heard the door opening. But she stayed, as immobile as a statue, for just a fraction of a second before turning her head to greet her guests.

'Natasha, darling! How lovely to see you!' She wore some kind of turban on her head, in an orange fabric a few shades darker than her fringed 1920s bob. The long scarf that hung from it swung with the movement of her head, emphasising her cheekbones and sculptured jawline.

She stepped away from the fireplace, and the purple and orange silk of her pyjamas seemed to flow and swirl as she moved. With a laugh, Natasha came away from the door and into the room, skirting the table to reach her hostess.

Grace felt Kai's hand at the small of her back, and he gave her a gentle push into the room, taking her away from the door which he closed behind him.

'Angela!' Swept into an embrace, Natasha kissed the older woman on both cheeks. 'It's great to be here. Thank you so much for inviting us. And you look marvellous. That hat is perfect with the pyjama suit. Where did you find it?'

Angela touched her hand to the back of her head.

'Paris. A simply fabulous little boutique off the Champs Elysées. Jane and Carla won't shop anywhere else. Jane Birkin, Carla Bruni,' she explained airily, looking across at Grace who stood near the door.

Kai was behind her, close though not touching, but she imagined she could still feel the imprint of his hand on her back through her padded jacket.

'Hi, I'm Natasha's sister. Grace.' She stepped forward, holding out her hand,

and found she too was swept into an embrace and kissed on both cheeks.

'Ye-es,' Angela said, holding Grace away and looking from her to Natasha and back again. 'I think I can see a slight family resemblance. Though you really are as different as chalk and cheese.' She laughed. 'Never mind. It's lovely to have you here with us, darling! Oh, and Kai darling!'

Letting go of Grace, she held out her arms and he stepped forward, wrapping his mother in a tight embrace.

'You're looking good,' he said when he finally released her. 'Everything OK?'

'Yes. You're looking tired, Kai.' There was concern in her eyes.

'Where's Vespasien?'

'Angela's husband?' Grace mouthed, looking at her sister. Natasha nodded.

'He'll be in the wine cellars,' Angela was saying.

'OK. I'll say bonjour later. I'm going to crash for a couple of hours.'

'I'm so sorry, darling. You sounded so angry with me when you phoned when you were rescuing our two damsels in distress here . . .'

He shrugged.

'I'd been hoping for a quiet time over Christmas, that's all.'

'I thought you wouldn't mind a few guests. Johnno and Barbs will be arriving this afternoon — weather permitting! Oh — and Cameron, of course.'

'Johnno and Barbs? Great,' Kai said, his tone devoid of all enthusiasm. 'I'll stay to say hello to Cameron. After that, I'm off.'

'No, Kai, you . . .'

But his expression was grim, Grace saw, and vying with the weariness that she sensed like a weight across his shoulders. He was clearly in no mood for discussion.

She wanted to murmur something soothing, give his hand a quick, comforting squeeze perhaps, but instead she watched in silence as he crossed to the door the three of them had come in by, grasped the handle of his case and wheeled it over to a door on the other side of the room. There he turned and looked from his mother to Natasha to Grace.

'Goodbye, ladies. I'll see you at lunch.'

He left, closing the door behind him, and for a moment there was silence in the kitchen.

'Well,' Angela said brightly, beaming a smile. 'You two won't need to carry your cases up. I've hired an aged retainer for the Christmas period. He'll do it.'

'An aged retainer?' It was such a delightfully quaint expression. Grace found she was laughing — with Angela, not at her, and wondered if that was what Angela had intended.

Angela was narcissistic and snobbish, but she knew it and could laugh at herself for it. It was impossible not to like someone who could do that, Grace realised.

'So, darlings,' Angela said, 'why don't we sit down and have coffee and croissants, and you and I, Natasha, can run through the arrangements for the fashion show tomorrow.'

* ★ *

The aged retainer was called Pierre and had an unlit roll-up stuck to his upper lip. His face, tanned and lined by a life spent outdoors, put him at somewhere between sixty and eighty.

He lifted their cases, one in each of his large countryman's hands, as if they weighed no more than a couple of chickens and took Grace and Natasha through to the entrance hall with its wide, polished stone staircase. A tall Christmas tree, decorated with gold bows and soft-glowing lights, stood at its foot.

The hall was vast and stretched up to the second floor. A stairwell on a grand scale, Grace decided, delighted to see the paintings — portraits of ancestors mainly — that lined the walls.

'No dawdling over the pictures,' Natasha said as they followed Pierre up the stairs.

Grace laughed.

'Another time,' she warned.

Their rooms were on the second floor,

facing west, next to each other with just a bathroom between them which they would share.

'What a view,' Grace breathed, crossing to the window of her sister's room and looking out.

The snow was still falling, and everything looked smooth, white, untouched — the park that stretched before them, the forest they'd driven through that Grace could see to her right, the gentle slopes of the hills on her left.

'Just think — Kai Curtis in the same house as us,' Natasha said. She'd put her suitcase on the bed and was taking her clothes out and arranging them carefully in the wardrobe. 'I can't believe Angela never said he was her son. Clever her, though, for telling us to bring just one present each. I mean, what would you get for someone like Kai Curtis?'

'Hmm, yes,' Grace murmured, her mind elsewhere. She'd been given the brief 'art collector, early fifties'. Johnno or Barbs, she now surmised. She'd found a signed limited-edition print by a contemporary artist that would, she hoped, be just right.

'Hey,' Natasha said. 'Which room's his, do you reckon? The room next door maybe,' she suggested, a hint of mischief in her tone, 'or the one next door to yours. What do you think?'

For a long moment, Grace couldn't respond. She stayed where she was by the window, gazing out, seeing nothing. The strong lines of Kai's face, the sheer physical presence of the man and, too, the weariness she'd glimpsed in him — all were so vivid in her mind.

So many things about him drew her to him in a way she'd never been drawn to a man before.

But she recalled the way he'd looked at her sister — her stunning sister — and knew he'd never be interested in her, Grace.

Expelling her breath on a shaky sigh, she found her voice at last.

'Let's not talk about him,' she said, turning away from the window. 'I'm going to unpack.' And she left, before the puzzled look that crossed Natasha's face could turn itself into a question.

As pre-arranged with Angela, at 12.30 they made their way downstairs for lunch. Reaching the first floor, Grace glanced to her left and saw Kai turn a corner and come towards them, and the breath caught in her throat.

He moved with an easy stride and looked wonderful, tall and lean in a dark grey shirt open at the neck and trousers the same colour belted low at the waist. He hadn't shaved, and a day's growth of beard shadowed his jaw. As he drew near, she breathed in the smoky notes of his cologne.

'You're looking good,' she said with a smile. 'Refreshed.'

'I am.' He smiled back.

She glanced at her sister, relieved to see Natasha's concentration was fixed on the sketchpad she held. She wouldn't have noticed the colour Grace was sure now warmed her cheeks.

'There you are, darlings.' It was Angela,

waiting at the foot of the stairs on the ground floor. 'All three of you, good. We're eating in the dining-room. Come and meet Vespasien, my husband.'

Natasha fell in with Angela while Grace and Kai followed behind. Although no doubt he'd have preferred to be with Natasha, she thought unhappily.

'Your mother's got some marvellous paintings,' she said, her gaze skimming portraits and landscapes as they walked along together.

'Actually, it's my stepfather who's the collector, not my mother.'

'Vespasien's family,' Angela put in, glancing behind her at the two of them, 'have been collecting great works of art for centuries.'

'Look, a Monet,' Grace said, pointing. 'An early Monet. Oh, and a Renoir. I love the Impressionists.'

'You certainly know your stuff,' Kai said.

'Yes, I — . . . Oh.' A painting half hidden by a vase of flowers had caught her eye. She stopped and leaned across the small table the vase stood on in order to have a closer look at it. 'It's signed 'Sisley 67'. 1867, of course. But there's something about the brushstrokes . . .' She frowned, voice trailing away.

'How clever of you to spot it, darling.' Angela had doubled back. Natasha stood just behind her. 'I sent it away to be restored, and . . .'

'Restored?' Natasha cut in. 'Oh, Grace could have done it for you.'

'Grace? I don't understand.'

'It's my job,' Grace said, conscious of Kai's unsmiling gaze on her face. 'I restore paintings for a living.'

She found herself frowning again as the four of them moved off, heading towards the dining-room. She'd hardly expected a gushing 'Oh, how exciting, darling!' But Angela's 'Oh. Yes. I wish I'd known' seemed strangely out of character. Far too low-key.

Winter Wonderland

Seated at the head of the table, Vespasien Beauvallon de Mottefort rose to his feet as Grace and her sister, and Kai and his mother entered the dining-room.

An Irish setter, its fur a rich dark red, lay stretched out on its side in front of the wide hearth where a log fire burned. It too jumped to its feet, long feathery tail swishing a heartfelt greeting.

'Loki, *assis*, sit.'

Kai's stepfather was tall, good-looking, and impeccably groomed, his style of dress as unique in its way as his wife's — waistcoat and plus-fours in dark brown corduroy, a soft linen shirt buttoned up to the neck, no tie.

Brown and white two-tone brogues over knee-high socks completed the outfit. His hair was cut short and held no trace of grey though he had to be in his fifties or early sixties.

The total effect was original and, yes, very French, Grace decided.

He shook her hand, then Natasha's, with an '*Enchanté, mademoiselle,*' each time.

'Come and sit down. Make yourselves at home. Do.' He spoke English with a charming accent.

He turned to look at his stepson.

'No time to shave, Kai?' he murmured.

His tone was one of mild enquiry, but Grace saw Angela, walking down to the other end of the table, pause for the briefest of moments.

Kai smiled.

'That's right,' he replied in an equally mild tone.

Angela continued on to the end of the table. They all took their places, and Grace wondered if she'd been mistaken. Perhaps that moment of tension had never occurred.

A tree, smaller than the one in the hall, stood in one corner. Decorated with pomanders and slices of dried fruit, it filled the room with the scents of pine, oranges, and cloves.

Lunch was a light meal — soup with

yeasty homemade bread warm from the oven, followed by a colourful selection of satsumas, kakis and lychees, bright pink in their shell-like skins — all of it washed down with a bottle of Château Beauvallon red.

'Two thousand and five vintage,' Vespasien said, raising his glass. 'One of the best years ever.'

Conversation was lively, and there was much laughter. Sitting opposite Kai, Grace found her gaze drawn to him time after time. She could watch his mobile features for ever, she thought, loving the way his mouth broadened into a grin, eyes crinkling at the corners, when he laughed.

For the time being at least he looked relaxed, the weight of weariness gone from his shoulders, and she was happy for him.

Every now and then his eyes met hers, and her breath would catch. It was as if they were in a world of their own, a special world for just the two of them.

But those moments were short, and

Grace knew they didn't mean anything.

'It's not usually like this, darlings,' Angela was saying. 'I do most of the cooking round here when there's just the two of us. But with a houseful of guests over Christmas . . .' She swept the long trailing scarf of her turban over her shoulder.

'She has hired Pierre's wife, daughter and grandson to cook and serve the meals,' Vespasien said. Something in his tone belied his neutral expression.

'Vespasien still hasn't forgiven me for being so extravagant. Have you, darling?'

Her husband shot her a look and didn't reply. Loki growled in his sleep, tail giving the floor one single thump.

'I know,' Angela trilled brightly into the awkward silence. 'Why don't you show our guests round the wine cellars this afternoon? Later on, when Johnno and Barbs get here.'

Kai swore under his breath.

'Count me out,' he said, scraping his chair back across the tiled floor and standing up.

'You could do a wine-tasting, Vespi.' Angela turned to Grace and Natasha. 'What do you say, girls?'

Grace looked at her sister and nodded.

'That would be lovely.'

Vespasien too stood up.

'And I'll be delighted to show you how we make our wine here. Shall we say four o'clock?'

* * *

'Magical.' Closing the huge wooden entrance door behind her, Grace stood for a moment at the top of the double flight of steps that led up to it and took several long deep breaths.

It had stopped snowing, and the air was cold but still. The afternoon sun shone low in the sapphire sky, casting long shadows and glinting off ice crystals in the snow.

There was indeed a fairy-tale sense of magic in the scene before her, Grace thought.

She was alone. Angela had announced at the end of lunch that she and Vespasien were going to have their usual short siesta.

Grace and her sister, helped by the aged retainer Pierre and his daughter Séverine, had carried the clothes for the fashion show along to a room off the grand salon. The two of them had then spent some time in Grace's room sending messages to their parents and friends.

'Best not to say anything about Kai Curtis being here,' Grace had cautioned.

'Shame,' her sister retorted with a laugh. 'We're sitting on the scoop of the century.'

Shortly afterwards, tired after the drive in difficult conditions, Natasha had gone to have a lie down in her room.

Grace had thought of asking Kai if he'd like to accompany her on a walk. But, aware she might be motivated by more than a simple wish for his company, she'd shied away from the idea. Besides, she hadn't known where to find him.

Someone had cleared the steps. Grace

ran lightly down them before striking out to her right where the snow lay smooth and pristine.

She walked parallel to the front of the château, smiling at the various sets of bird tracks she saw. Once, she caught sight of something larger, the hooves of a deer perhaps, or a boar. She didn't see a single human footprint, though. She could have been the only person in the whole of France.

She rounded the corner of the château — and stopped dead in her tracks.

Kai. Some ten metres away, his tall dark silhouette a sharp contrast to the white of the snow. He had his back to her, the binoculars he was holding to his eyes trained on the forest they'd driven through earlier that day. The trees came close to the château at this point.

He must have heard her or seen her out of the corner of his eye. Abruptly, he lowered the binoculars, twisting round to look at her.

A look of irritation flashed across his face.

'Are you following me?'

'Of course not.' Grace bristled at the unfairness of the accusation. Looking beyond him, she saw a trail of footprints in the snow. He must have let himself out through the kitchen and come round the back of the château. 'If I'd known you were here,' she said icily, 'and didn't want company — I'd have gone in the opposite direction.'

For a long moment, he didn't react. His eyes stayed on her, his expression hard, unyielding. Then she saw the tension ease from his shoulders. His mouth sketched a bleak smile.

'I'm sorry. There was no call for me to speak to you like that.' He drew in a breath. 'Come and see what I've been looking at.'

'Oh.' Intrigued, Grace crossed the few metres between them. His fingers brushed hers as he handed her the binoculars and, even though he, like her, wore leather gloves, she found her heart skittering into a fast, insistent beat.

She could smell his cologne, and the

leather of his coat, mingling with the scent of woodsmoke in the air. He was too close, she thought, stepping back a pace.

'Where do I look?'

'Over there, at the base of the treeline. You see the tree that's fallen over? OK, left a bit. Slowly. You'll see a gap. Stop there.'

Following Kai's instructions, Grace looked through the binoculars at the gap in the trees. At first she could make nothing out, but when she did, her mouth formed an 'Oh' of wonder.

'Oh, wow. I can see deer. Three of them. Their eyes, their faces.' She gave a little laugh of delight. 'They're looking back at me.'

'Keeping a wary eye on you,' Kai corrected, and she could hear laughter in his voice. 'On you and me both.'

Grace lowered the binoculars and turned to look at him. His face had a healthier colour than before, and his stance was relaxed. Yes, relaxed and happy.

'You love it here in France at the château, don't you?' she said.

'It's one of the few places I can be myself.'

'Yes. I can understand that,' she said, and there was a breathlessness in her voice. Here was a man rather more complex than the bad-boy portrayed in the tabloids, she thought. 'You top the charts time after time. Every song's a number one hit. But fame and success aren't all they're cracked up to be, I guess.'

She saw him tense, eyes narrowing as he looked at her face. As though suspecting mockery, perhaps. Then his shoulders eased, and she knew what he'd seen in her expression had reassured him. He'd accepted her words at face value.

'You're right. They're not,' he said, his tone telling her to drop the subject. He gestured towards the trees. 'Walk with me.'

They moved off, side by side, heading at an angle towards the treeline. That way, Grace supposed, they wouldn't disturb the deer they'd seen. It was several degrees colder here, in the shadow cast by the trees, and her breath — and Kai's — hovered white in the still air. The snow scrunched beneath her boots.

She tried to imagine what it was like to be as famous as Kai Curtis. People must recognise him wherever he went. At the shops, the cinema, if he went out for a meal — all the things she, Grace, and everyone else took for granted would have ceased to hold any pleasure for him.

Screaming fans would come running up to him, clamouring for a selfie. Or he'd have to dodge the paparazzi eager to catch him out at an unguarded moment.

No doubt he'd loved every minute of it when he first became famous — travelling the world, living a life of luxury, pursued by adoring fans. But even adulation, she decided, must become tiresome after a while.

She must have made a sound, some tiny inward pitying sound, for he looked sharply at her.

'What is it?'

'The paparazzi. I've just realised, there

aren't any paparazzi here at the château. They don't know where you are, do they?'

'No-one does. Not even my manager.'

'You've escaped.' It wasn't a question.

'I had to.'

How long, Grace wondered, and her heart was full of sadness for him. How long before someone rang the château to see if he was there? How many days of freedom would he manage to grab before then?

They came to the treeline and took a narrow, gently twisting path, barely discernible beneath the snow. A blackbird called in alarm as it swooped low past them. A few metres further on, Kai pointed to the ground.

'Deer.'

Grace looked down to see hoof-prints, each one like two long thin parallel ovals, some partly covering others, cutting across from one side of their path to the other.

'Can you tell how many?'

Smiling, Kai shook his head.

About to move off again, he put out his arm, staying her. A tension about him told her to say nothing. She looked where he was looking — and her heart stilled for an instant.

It was a squirrel, no more than five metres away. A red squirrel, she realised, though its coat had a greyish tinge to it. Smaller than the greys she was used to back home, the animal sat on its haunches at the base of a tree, nibbling at the nut it held between its front paws.

Grace stood stock-still, hardly daring to breathe, her whole being caught up in the wonder of the moment. The squirrel's tail was all fluffed up, and its ears were long and tufty, just like those of squirrels in the picture books she'd read as a child. She'd never seen such a beautiful animal.

All at once it stopped eating. Ears perked, it remained motionless for a fraction of a second before dropping the nut, twisting round and darting up the tree, all in one swift, nimble movement.

Grace watched until it was out of sight

before turning to Kai. A broad smile, she was sure, lit her whole face.

'That was amazing. He was just so cute!'

'You sound like a two-year-old, not a twenty-something.' But he too was smiling, and Grace knew the comment wasn't meant unkindly.

'They don't hibernate?'

He shook his head.

'No, not in this part of France.'

As of one accord, they moved off again, following the path as it curved round to the right, heading back to the château.

'So you restore paintings for a living,' Kai said.

'That's right. I work for a smallish firm just outside London, and I love it,' she said, conscious her face was lighting up as it always did when she spoke about her job.

'Go on.'

'I love art — full stop,' she said with a laugh. 'But I love the variety, too. I could be cleaning years and years of grime off a painting, or re-varnishing it, or repairing and re-gilding a frame. There are never two weeks the same.'

'I imagine you have to be well qualified to do the job.'

She shrugged.

'I've got a degree in art history and a master's in art conservation.'

An eyebrow went up.

'Impressive. Tell me,' he went on, 'what was it about the Sisley painting that worried you?'

'The Sisley painting?' she echoed, playing for time. It wasn't the abrupt switch that now disconcerted her. No, it was something about his tone. All at once she was seized with the notion that this was why he'd asked her to walk with him.

'Yes,' he said. 'I saw your face when you first spotted it. You frowned. Something wasn't quite right.'

'Well, yes. It's been restored, but rather unevenly.' Grace paused an instant, gathering her thoughts. 'In his early work, Sisley tended to favour dark, sombre colours — drab olives, greys and browns. But the restorer seems to have overpainted in places, adding a green that's just a shade too bright.'

'Do restorers normally do that? Over-paint? Would you do that?'

'Not unless I had to. And there's another thing . . .'

'Yes?'

'The brushstrokes. Nice soft brush-strokes, giving a lovely misty feel to the trees. But the lane — it almost looks as if it was painted a decade or so later.'

'The restorer painting over the original again?'

'Must be.' She drew in a breath before continuing. 'I think very few people would have been able to spot the things that weren't quite right. It takes a trained eye.'

'Like yours.'

'Yes.'

'I see.'

The path had brought them close to the edge of the trees. Grace could see the snow-covered expanse of the château park and, beyond, the creamy-coloured walls of the château itself.

They'd almost reached the open ground when Kai stopped and turned to face her, catching her gloved hand in his.

'I want to thank you,' he said, 'for not asking too many questions.'

Her heart gave a painful thump. How she longed to reach up and touch her fingertips to his beard-shadowed jaw.

'While answering all yours,' she said with a smile. The breathlessness was back in her voice.

'Yes.' His gaze held hers, and when he drew her closer and bent to touch his lips to hers in the lightest of kisses, it seemed the most natural thing in the world.

Stab of Envy

'All pedigree dogs born in 2015,' Vespasien Beauvallon de Mottefort was saying in his near-perfect English, 'have names beginning with L.'

It was just past four, and the three of them — Kai's stepfather, Grace and Natasha — were heading for the wine cellars and the promised wine-tasting. Johnno and Barbs had phoned to say problems with their hire car meant they'd be delayed.

'So a dog born in 2016 . . .' Grace said, 'will have a name beginning with M.'

'Exactly.'

They were in the walkway that led from the kitchen to the barn where the cars were housed. Loki trotted along beside his master, the long silky fur of his tail sweeping happily from side to side.

Vespasien opened the door to the barn and stood back to usher the two sisters through. He gestured across to the far end of the building.

'You see those tractors over there? Narrow, with the operator's cab high up off the ground? Well, they're specially designed so that the wheels go either side of a single row of vines.'

'Ah, yes,' Natasha said. 'Grace thought they were something to do with wine-making.'

'*Très bien*.'Vespasien beamed at the two sisters. 'Follow me, please.' He crossed to the huge wooden doors they'd driven in through that morning. The doors she'd helped Kai close, Grace thought, the image of him with snowflakes in his hair uncomfortably vivid in her mind.

A normal-sized door had been built in to the right-hand door. Vespasien unbolted it, and the three of them stepped through and set off in the direction of a large building on the other side of the courtyard.

Loki bounded away, running ahead, circling back, running off again, clearly loving being out in the snow.

The sun had sunk below the treeline and Grace shivered in the cold, glad of the padded jacket she wore over her thick sweater and jeans — glad, too, of her fleece-lined ankle boots which made walking through snow relatively easy.

She saw her sister, stunning as always in her full-length coat, Dr Zhivago-style hat and high-heeled boots place each footstep with care.

'Are you OK?' she asked, concern in her voice.

Natasha shot her a tight smile.

'Fine, thanks.'

Like the barn that served as a garage, the wine cellars had tall wooden doors with a smaller door set into the right-hand one. Vespasien took a key out of the pocket of the camel-coloured overcoat he wore, unlocked the door and ushered them inside. A heady mix of alcohol and grape juice assailed Grace's nostrils.

'We're using the back way in,' Vespasien said. 'That way, you can see the process, how the wine is made, from start to finish, and we'll end up in my office where you can taste some of the wines. How does that sound?'

'Perfect,' Natasha said. 'It sounds perfect.'

'So, the grapes come in here, and first they're sorted in this machine here.' He indicated a wide stainless-steel contraption, shiny and gleamingly clean in the harsh electric light, as indeed was everything else Grace could see around her.

Loki had stayed outside, rooting around in the snow. No doubt he was forbidden to come inside the cellars.

'And last year's vintage is maturing in these vats,' Vespasien was saying. It was half an hour or so later, and they were nearing the end of their tour and now stood in front of huge stainless-steel containers, each twice as tall as a man.

'All the time the wine is in these vats, it's improving in quality and flavour. We'll bottle it at the end of the winter.'

It had been no surprise that Vespasien Beauvallon de Mottefort was a knowledgeable guide, and normally Grace enjoyed and appreciated listening to an expert in any particular field.

But this afternoon was different. It was lucky her sister had asked lots of questions because Grace had remained largely silent, her mind drifting constantly to thoughts of Kai.

What was he doing now, she wondered. After that kiss that was no kiss, he'd held her hand a moment longer as he drew away from her. And there'd been something strange about the way he'd looked at her. As though all at once he was seeing her in a different light.

As they headed towards the château, she'd thrown his question back at him.

'So what is it about the Sisley painting that worries you?'

He didn't answer straight away, but his expression was grim.

'I wish I knew,' he'd said at last. He let her in through a door that opened on to the rear of the entrance hall. 'Maybe I'll see you at dinner,' he said, and she watched him walk away with that easy stride of his, then take the stairs two by two.

Before going upstairs herself, she'd

made for the corridor that led to the dining-room to check that her first impressions of the Sisley were correct. But the painting had gone.

And that was odd, she thought now, coming back to the present with a jolt to see Natasha disappear through a door. Vespasien stood by the doorway, obviously waiting for Grace to follow.

His office was both a workroom and a showcase. A bar counter ran the length of the wall on Grace's left. Bottles of wine, grouped in threes or fives, were displayed at intervals along it.

At the far end, she could see the door by which people who only wanted to taste or buy wine would come in. On her right was the business side of the room — a desk and office chair, a laptop and printer, papers and other documents neatly stacked.

Grace wandered round, captivated by the displays on the walls — photos of a proud, smiling Vespasien being handed a cup or a medal, certificates in frames showing the awards Château Beauvallon wines had received, old black and white photos revealing the clothes and equipment of yesteryear.

'Fascinating,' she murmured. Natasha, she saw, had taken out her sketchpad and pencil.

At the desk, a pile of wine bottle labels caught her eye. She picked them up. The name — Château Beauvallon — together with the pen-and-ink drawing of part of the château's façade and the year — 2005 — were self-explanatory. But Grace's schoolgirl French could make little sense of the rest. She looked round. 'Vespasien . . .'

He was standing behind the bar counter, a bottle in one hand, corkscrew in the other, intent on his task. He looked up, and something close to anger darkened his face.

'Put those labels down.'

Grace recoiled as if stung. Natasha, startled, glanced up from her sketchpad and looked with wide eyes from Grace to Vespasien.

'I'm sorry,' he said, coming round from

behind the counter, 'I didn't mean to be so abrupt.' Swiftly crossing the room, he took the labels from her, opened a drawer in the desk and slipped them inside. 'We have to keep the labels as good as new. We try not to handle them too much.'

'I'm the one who should apologise,' Grace said, her pulse slowing to its usual rhythm, 'but I was just wondering if you could explain the wording on a label?'

'Yes, of course. But first I'll teach you how to taste wine.'

How? Intrigued, Grace moved with him over to the bar counter and Natasha, and watched as he pulled the cork on a bottle of Château Beauvallon red and poured the wine into three long-stemmed glasses. He handed the sisters a glass each.

'Raise the glass,' he said, following his own instructions, 'and look at the colour. Is it a good, rich colour? In this case, yes — of course,' he added with a smile. 'Now, bring the glass to your nose and inhale. What can you smell?'

Silence. She'd never thought about

it before, she realised. What could she smell?

'Fruit. I can smell fruit.'

'Good. And is your mouth starting to water?'

Both sisters nodded.

'Now take some wine. Don't swallow it. Keep it in your mouth and chew it, as if you're chewing an apple or a peach. Like this.'

Natasha giggled. Grace giggled too. It was crazy — she was rolling a mouthful of wine over her tongue and round her teeth, making the sort of unladylike slurping noises children might make to annoy their parents.

'Swallow just a little at a time,' Vespasien instructed, 'and breathe as you swallow. Take your time.'

And it was working. There was an intensity of flavour in her mouth that she'd never experienced before, Grace thought, pleasantly surprised.

'We'll taste this one next,' Vespasien continued in his lightly accented English. 'A 2016 white.'

In the end, Grace and Natasha ordered a case of red and one of white which they'd share between them when they returned home.

Night had fallen by the time the two of them made their way up the steps to the château's main entrance. Vespasien wasn't with them. He was taking Loki for a walk.

Apart from that odd little hiccup over the labels, Grace reflected, it had all been very enjoyable and they'd learned a lot. For some reason, though, she was uneasy. Something was niggling away at the back of her brain. Something about the missing Sisley?

★ ★ ★

'You look lovely, Grace. You really do.' Natasha's tone was reassuring and clearly sincere. She stood behind and a little to one side of her sister, both of them studying Grace's reflection in the full-length mirror in her room.

Grace had put on one of her sister's

clever designs. It looked like a dress but was in fact two pieces — a skirt and a long-sleeved boat-necked top — both made from the same soft, free-flowing fabric.

'You're like me,' Natasha said. 'With your hair and complexion you can wear strong colours. That deep pinky-red, yes, it looks good on you. Don't forget to do lots of swirls,' she added, mischief in her tone.

They were dressing for dinner which, they'd been told before they came over to France, was always a formal affair when there were guests.

Natasha looked, as always, beautiful in a knee-length fitted dress in a black and white leopard print.

Grace flipped her phone open, saw the time, and drew in a long breath.

'Let's head on down.'

Why was she so nervous, she asked herself as they made their way along the corridor and down the stairs. Then she recalled the way Kai had joined them earlier as they went down to lunch, and it occurred to her that that was why — she wanted him to notice her, and the sheer stupidity of the notion was frightening. For why would he notice her when her beautiful sister was close by?

'This way, darlings. We're having apé-ritifs in the petit salon first. Come and meet Johnno and Barbs.'

Angela had stayed with her 1920s theme, Grace saw. Tonight she wore feathers in her hair and long strings of pearls over a black and cream mid-calf-length dress. Lipstick and nail varnish matched her hair.

Vespasien, in a nut brown three-piece suit and bright yellow bow-tie, looked understated by comparison.

The petit salon was warm and softly lit. The metre-length logs that burned in the wide fireplace were more for atmos-phere than effect, Grace had discovered, glad of the efficient heating system that kept the château snug and dry. Displays of creamy-white mistletoe, glossy holly berries and golden rosehips added to the festive Christmas atmosphere.

'I dabble in antiques. And fine art. Based in Brighton. Wintersley's. You might have heard of me,' Johnno Wintersley said airily, no doubt expecting the answer 'Ah, yes'.

He'd given Grace and her sister a kiss, French-style, on both cheeks even though he'd never met either of them before, and had now somehow managed to corral the two of them into one corner of the room.

His expensive aftershave failed to disguise the odour of cigarettes that clung to his clothes, and Grace couldn't help hoping he'd disappear some time soon to have a smoke. Now she understood why Kai had been so dismayed on hearing Johnno Wintersley would be staying at the château.

'Excuse me,' she said, 'Angela needs our help.'

'Does she? I can't see her,' Johnno said, clearly puzzled.

Ignoring him, Grace took Natasha's hand and the two of them slipped away past him.

'Naughty,' Natasha chided, laughing.

'I couldn't stand the man a moment longer.' Grace sucked in a shaky breath. Kai wasn't there and she was hard put to hide her disappointment. The room seemed empty without him.

Angela came in carrying a tray of tall narrow glasses.

'Kir royale, darlings. Help yourselves. And take one to Barbs over there, will you?'

Grace lifted two of the glasses from the tray. The wine they contained was suffused with a soft pink blush. Streams of tiny bubbles shot to the surface. She brought one of the glasses to her nose.

'I can smell raspberries.'

Angela beamed at her.

'Spot on! Sparkling wine and raspberry liqueur. Delicious.'

Barbs Wintersley, thankfully, was a complete contrast to her husband.

'Angela and I were at school together. Best friends. So of course we've known each other for years. She says you're a brilliant dress designer, Natasha. . . '

With that, the two women fell into a happy discussion of the dress Natasha was wearing, the outfit Grace was wearing and the colours that would suit Barbs.

Grace sipped her kir, smiled a lot, did a twirl when asked, but her mind was elsewhere. What was Kai doing? Was he happy — or deeply unhappy, pacing up and down or pounding the walls with frustration because guests had invaded the place where he found sanctuary?

Something, some sixth sense perhaps, made her glance across the room — and there he was, standing in the doorway, and her breath caught in her throat.

He'd dressed for the occasion and looked magnificent in black jacket and trousers, bright white shirt and black bow-tie. The shadow of beard had gone, accentuating the sculptured quality of the strong lines of his face.

He was looking at her, the hint of a smile curving his lips. But his gaze flicked to Natasha and on to Barbs, and Grace realised with a pang that it was pure coincidence. He'd happened to have been looking at her at the same instant she'd glanced over at the door.

With an inaudible sigh, she turned her attention back to Natasha and Barbs, watching from the corner of her eye as Kai crossed the room to join Vespasien and Loki by the fireplace.

Shortly afterwards, the party moved through double doors into the dining-room. Loki lay down and stretched out in front of the fire while his master took his usual seat at the head of the long rectangular table. Grace was placed on his left, with Barbs opposite her.

Kai sat diagonally opposite — with Natasha talking in a low voice to him on his right, Grace saw, not liking the stab of envy that twisted inside her.

Sévérine and another woman brought in the starter — a tangy cream cheese and smoked salmon concoction on a bed of salad leaves — and Vespasien opened a bottle of white wine.

'So where's Cameron, Angie?' Johnno, on Grace's left, said. 'I thought he'd be here for Christmas.'

'Angela. Call me Angela, please.' Kai's mother sat on the other side of Johnno, which meant Grace couldn't see her face. But she heard the sharpness in her tone.

'Kai's brother,' Barbs supplied, for Grace's benefit.

'He's in Paris,' Vespasien said, pouring himself a glass of wine. 'He's got a lady friend there.'

There was something odd about the way Kai looked across the table at Angela, and Grace wished she could see the older woman's face. She only heard her words.

'But he'll be here tomorrow. Tomorrow morning, darlings.'

'So what have you got planned for us all, Angela?' Barbs asked.

'We-ell, tomorrow afternoon's the fashion show, of course. We'll be doing the final preparations in the morning. Séverine's daughter and two of her friends will be here at ten, Natasha darling. Lovely girls, tall and willowy. No experience of the catwalk but full of enthusiasm.'

Vespasien rolled his eyes.

'Sounds horrendous. If you need me tomorrow, I'll be in the wine cellars. All day.'

'Think I'll join you, Vesp,' Johnno said.

'What can I do to help?' Kai asked in his deep growl of a voice.

'The sound system, Kai darling. The music, the amplifiers . . . things like that.'

'Grace can help with that,' Natasha put in. 'She's the practical one out of us two.'

Thanks a bunch, Grace thought, conscious of the colour that swept over her face when Kai turned his head to send her a long look.

'We'll have an early-ish lunch,' Angela continued. 'Our guests will start arriving about one, and the show will start at two. Pierre's cousin operates the snow plough for the commune. He'll make sure the road's clear.'

'Wonderful,' Barbs enthused.

Kai and Natasha were deep in conversation, Grace saw, biting her lip.

'Costing me a fortune,' Vespasien grumbled, so low Grace suspected she wasn't meant to hear.

Angela went on to detail the programme for the rest of their stay — a murder mystery evening the day after the fashion show, the traditional big meal — the Réveillon — the evening of Christmas Eve, and church followed by a quiet winding-down on Christmas Day itself.

The evening progressed. Grace listened and laughed, she ate the delicious food, drank the delicious wine, joined in all the talk. Time after time, though, she found her gaze drawn across the table to Kai and her sister. Heads close, they were clearly engrossed in each other.

So he found her beautiful, talented sister attractive. What was so surprising about that? Natasha worked hard and had had little time to devote to relationships. But a romance with Kai, even a short-lived fling, might be just what her sister needed.

Think positive thoughts, Grace told herself. But the notion did little to ease her unhappiness.

What's Not to Like?

'I'm so nervous,' Natasha said, crossing Grace's bedroom and sitting on the edge of her bed. She'd left open the door to the bathroom that separated their two rooms, and light from it spilled into the bedroom.

'Oh Nat, love.' Blinking, Grace pushed herself into an upright position. She'd been in that warm, drowsy halfway state, somewhere between being asleep and being awake, and in her sleeping daydream she'd been in Kai's arms. 'It'll be fine. You've done fashion shows before.'

Natasha's eyes flashed in the yellow light.

'You're always so sensible. So down-to-earth. Yes, I've done fashion shows before. At college. That doesn't stop me being nervous now.'

'Hey,' Grace said gently, taking both her sister's hands in hers. 'Your clothes are fabulous. You're fabulous. The setting for the show is amazing — and you've got

71

a whole load of wealthy women coming here, just itching to spend their money.'

Natasha laughed and pulled a rueful face.

'I'm sorry. You're right, and I shouldn't have snapped at you.'

Grace was proud of her sister. Natasha worked hard and deserved every bit of success that came her way. She had a small niche boutique in the Lanes in Brighton that she'd built up from scratch, designing and making gorgeous clothes, especially wedding and evening dresses. Her list of moneyed clients never stopped growing, and her website was flourishing.

Natasha sucked in a breath, then expelled it slowly.

'This could send my career in a whole new direction. If I get lots of orders, I'll need to take on more staff.'

'More staff?'

Another laugh, lighter this time.

'OK, staff, full stop.' Up till now in her career, she'd had people she could call on at busy times but no-one permanently on her payroll. She grew serious. 'And it's not just me. Angela has a lifestyle to keep up. She needs the commission.'

'Vespasien muttered something about her extravagance at lunch yesterday, didn't he?' Grace murmured.

'A place like this must cost a fortune to keep going. Maintaining the grounds, keeping the buildings in a good state of repair, redecorating, not to mention the day-to-day bills.'

'Yes, but the Château Beauvallon vineyards are the best in the region. They must earn quite a lot from the wine side of things.'

Natasha shrugged.

'Maybe. I think Kai's put quite a lot of money into the place,' she added after a moment.

'What?' Grace shook her head. 'Even if he has, he'd never tell you something like that, surely.'

'No. He didn't. But I reckon he helps his mother out financially. On the quiet, though. He probably wouldn't want Vespasien to know.' She smiled. 'I'm just reading between the lines. Something he said last night.'

Last night.

'You and Kai were getting on like a house on fire,' Grace said, hard put to hide the envy that swelled her throat. In her dreams, she'd been the one sitting next to him, looking into his eyes, smiling, happy simply because she was with him.

'Grace!' Natasha was staring at her sister, eyes wide with concern. 'You twerp,' she said, giving Grace's hands a squeeze. 'It's not what you're thinking. Why do you think I said you'd help Kai with the music?'

'To point out the contrast between plodding, practical me and wonderful, creative you?' Grace suggested, hating, but unable to prevent, the resentment and cattiness she heard in her voice.

'Idiot. You don't plod.' Another squeeze of the hands. 'He doesn't fancy me, if that's what you're thinking.'

'No?'

'No. Well, maybe he does.' Another

light laugh. 'But last night he talked about his brother, about the music I wanted for the show — and he talked about you,' she added, dropping the words in lightly, one by one, a smile on her face.

'Me? What did he say about me?'

Natasha jumped to her feet, letting go Grace's hands. The smile on her face was broader, full of mischief.

'Ask him yourself.' She pulled back the duvet. 'Come on, get up. It's my big day. We need to shower, get dressed, go downstairs and get busy.'

As Natasha disappeared into the bathroom, Grace looked at her phone. Seven thirty. And she found she was humming as she got out of bed, drew back the curtains and opened the shutters, quickly closing the windows when icy air fell into the room, chilling her skin and filling her lungs. It was one of Kai's hits she was humming. Not the latest. The one before that.

Day hadn't yet broken, and the sky was a slate grey starless mass that might or might not presage snow.

Humming still, she looked out over the grounds. Had it snowed again overnight? The trees didn't move. Nothing moved. The scene before her was so smooth and untroubled she could have been looking at a painting.

Yes, she thought, still humming when she and Natasha ran down the stairs, following the scent of coffee and fresh bread baking as they made for the kitchen and breakfast, Kai had got well and truly under her skin. She was looking forward to the time she'd spend with him, helping him with the sound system. And she might just ask him what he'd said to Natasha about her.

★　★　★

The two sisters had just started breakfast when Kai's brother Cameron arrived. From the enclosed walkway outside came the sound of footsteps approaching rapidly, then the low iron-studded door swung open and he ducked his head as he came into the kitchen.

'Brr, it's cold out there,' he said, beaming a smile at Grace and Natasha. 'Just the two of you here?'

Two or three years younger and not quite so tall, with his dark hair and strong-boned face he was unmistakably Kai's brother. He was dressed as impeccably as his stepfather Vespasien always was, although his style was far more casual — a thick jacket, its wide collar pulled up around his ears, narrow-legged jeans and ankle-high trainers.

'I'm Cameron,' he said, pulling off his jacket and throwing it over the back of one of the chairs. 'And you're . . . ?'

'Natasha,' Grace's sister said, holding out her hand.

'Ah, so you must be Grace.'

The way his gaze lingered over her face, as if studying her features, for just a fraction of a second longer than was comfortable, was puzzling — and unnerving.

'I hear you went all woozy over a squirrel,' he said.

Woozy? All at once she understood. Hot colour washed over her cheeks. Kai must have phoned or texted his brother about her. What had he said? And why? To poke fun at her?

With an effort she brought a smile to her lips.

'He was very cute.'

'The squirrel or my brother?' Cameron laughed. 'Hey, don't answer that. So what have we got for breakfast?' he said, sitting down next to Natasha, opposite Grace. 'I'm starving.'

They passed round flaky, butter-rich croissants, still warm from the oven, homemade apricot jam and creamy unsalted butter while Cameron poured coffee into cups as big as soup bowls.

'No-one else down yet?' he asked, dropping sugar cubes into his coffee.

Grace shook her head.

'We haven't seen anyone.'

'Though two people have already had their breakfast,' Natasha said, gesturing towards two crumb-covered plates at the far end of the table.

'Hey, great detective work, Natasha,' Cameron said with a light laugh that robbed the remark of all possible offence. 'Let's hope Vespasien's been and gone,' he went on. 'I spend a lot of time in my studio when I'm here. Avoiding him. Keeping a low profile.'

'Studio?' Grace asked. Cameron was fun and made her smile, and she found she was intrigued and wanted to learn more about his relationship with his stepfather. But it seemed safer to stick with the more neutral topic.

'Has no-one told you I'm an artist?' His eyebrows shot up. 'I'm amazed. Maybe it's because I'm not much good!'

'Oh, I'm sure . . .' Natasha began.

'My work's been shown in a couple of galleries in Paris, though,' he said, 'so it can't be that bad.' He paused, eyes narrowing as he looked at Grace. 'You've got such a good face, you know. Not classically beautiful. But interesting. With that flawless skin and your striking hair, I can see you in a Rossetti painting.'

'Why, thank you.'

'Hey, I might have to paint you myself.'

Grace laughed.

'I think I might enjoy . . .'

She broke off as the internal door opened. Kai walked in — and her heart skittered into a faster beat. He wore a grey and white striped shirt and dark grey trousers, and looked magnificent. But then did he ever look anything other than magnificent, she asked herself.

'Cameron. Thought I could hear you chattering away. Grace, Natasha,' he murmured with a quick nod of greeting as he came away from the door. His brother stood up and moved round the table, and they met in a warm hug. There was clearly a great deal of affection between the two of them.

They drew apart and looked each other up and down.

'You're looking good, Cam.'

'Not sure I can say the same about you, mate. You're looking a bit ragged round the edges.'

Kai's smile was brief, meaningless.

'It's been tough. My heart's not in it any more.'

'But things might be about to change?'

Kai shrugged.

'We'll see. Long journey?' he went on.

'It was OK. All the roads have been cleared.'

'Vespasien said you'd been visiting a lady friend in Paris.'

A slow grin spread over Cameron's face.

'Did he now?'

There was amusement in Kai's eyes too, Grace saw, and all at once she understood: not a lady friend in Paris. A boyfriend.

She didn't know whether to be pleased or dismayed when Kai sat down beside her, opposite his brother. Passing him the basket of croissants, she breathed in the smoky notes of his cologne and the scent of freshly laundered clothes and watched his fine-boned hands as he poured himself coffee and refilled her cup.

In many respects she was the luckiest woman alive. Millions of fans would give their eye-teeth to be sitting where she was now. But what Cameron had said about the squirrel incident was casting its shadow over her. The notion that Kai might have been laughing about her was almost impossible to bear.

Hearing Natasha ask Cameron a question about Paris, she swallowed.

'I guess I behaved like an idiot yesterday, going all gaga over a squirrel,' she said.

'Going all . . . ?' He turned his head and looked at her, and Grace could see the flecks of gold in his brown eyes. 'On the contrary,' he said. 'It was lovely to see your face.'

She saw him hesitate, as though deciding whether to continue or not.

'It's something we share,' he said, 'that sense of wonder at the natural world. Don't ever lose it.'

His gaze held hers, Cameron and Natasha's voices faded to a murmur, and for the space of a heartbeat it was as if only he and she existed. The breath caught in her throat, and she wished the moment could go on for ever.

'I won't,' she promised.

Less than an hour later, and everyone was gathering in the grand salon, a magnificent room, the size of a small parish hall, and perfect for the fashion show.

The ceiling was high and decorated with intricate plasterwork and paintings of nymphs and goddesses from Greek mythology.

The walls were panelled in eau-de-nil silk that gleamed softly in the light from two huge chandeliers, while the floor was a warm polished oak parquet.

Tall arched windows on two sides let in a pale wintry light, and Grace imagined the curtains, abundant folds of fabric a shade darker than the walls, would be drawn closed for the afternoon's event.

A tall tree, decorated in glowing reds and golds, stood in one corner while long, trailing sprays of pine, holly and rosehips hung from the other three.

Natasha was talking earnestly to Marie-Laure who taught English in the local collège, Grace had learned.

Angela, resplendent in a full-length purple gown and matching turban, together with Vespasien in a Prince-of-Wales-checked three-piece suit, were sitting in armchairs upholstered in pale green silk, placed alongside what would become the catwalk.

Kai and Cameron were deep in conversation by one of the windows. Séverine and three other middle-aged French women stood in a group chatting while their menfolk stood in another group close by. They were all waiting for Pierre and his cousin to arrive.

Barbs would be a guest at the show that afternoon — Johnno, too, in the unlikely event he wanted to be present — so they weren't expected to help with the morning's preparations.

Grace moved across to the wall on her right and tried to study the paintings there. Portraits of ancestors, and well preserved.

Normally she never failed to enjoy studying the details of a painting, the details often brought back to light by the work of restorers such as herself. But today — today it was what Kai had said at the breakfast table that dominated her thoughts: so different in so many ways, yet the two of them had something in common, a passion they shared.

Pierre, unlit roll-up as usual stuck to his upper lip, came in with his cousin, carrying a gilded Louis XIV sofa between them which they deposited next to Angela. The meeting was complete.

Everyone gathered round Natasha. She cleared her throat.

'I'd like to thank you all for coming along to help with the preparations this morning.' She paused to allow Marie-Laure to translate. 'May I take this opportunity,' she continued, 'to thank Angela for coming up with the idea of a fashion show here, in this beautiful part of France, and Vespasien for so kindly agreeing to let us hold it in these splendid surroundings.'

A smattering of applause greeted her words. Grace could detect only the barest hint of nerves in Natasha's voice.

'You're doing great, Nat,' she muttered to herself, willing her sister on.

'The models will be arriving at ten,' Natasha said, 'so I'm just going to tell you what's happening because it's important you all know who's doing what.'

Grace only half-listened. She already knew her sister's plans for hairstyling, make-up, and the rehearsal scheduled for 11.30. She wasn't sure how it had happened, but Kai was standing next to her, and she was acutely aware of his closeness. She had only to move an inch or so and her arm would brush against his.

'Natasha darling . . .' Angela's imperious tone brought Grace's attention back to the meeting. 'My son must sing this afternoon. Just a couple of songs at the start and finish. It would be a total waste to do otherwise.' She turned to Kai. 'What do you say, darling?'

Grace had heard him swear under his breath, but he nodded.

'Of course. If Natasha would like me to.' No doubt he'd seen how Natasha, startled at first, was now beaming a smile of absolute delight.

'Need you ask! But, uh, the music for the show? Grace?'

Grace brought a smile to her face.

'No probs,' she said, biting back her disappointment as her dream of spending several hours in Kai's company vanished into the ether. 'I can handle the music.'

'Maybe Cameron can help you.'

'That layabout?' Vespasien, behind her, muttered scornfully, and she recalled Cameron's wish to avoid his stepfather. For good reason, it would seem.

She brought another bright smile to her face.

'It's all right, Nat. I can manage by myself, thanks.'

* * *

Shaking her head, Grace watched Vespasien disappear from view before she turned to Kai. It was some time later, the two of them were in a screened-off

87

section of the grand salon and she couldn't stop the feeling bubbling up inside her that all was right in her world after all.

She stood by a small table on which she'd placed her sister's laptop, and was running through the music Natasha had chosen for the show. To her surprise — and delight — Kai had brought in a chair and his guitar.

'Mind if I join you?'

He now sat less than a metre away, the ankle of one leg resting on the knee of the other as he tuned his guitar.

Beyond the silk-covered screens she could hear the excited chatter of many voices, the scrape of furniture being moved. And Vespasien had just threaded his way between the two screens, carrying the amplifier which he set down on the floor near the socket. She and Kai weren't alone by any means but it didn't matter. She was close to him — that was what mattered.

'Your stepfather doesn't seem to have a very high opinion of Cameron,' she said.

Kai glanced up.

'One, he hasn't got a proper job,' he said drily. 'Two, he doesn't pay anything towards his keep. Three, he's twenty-six but shows no sign of settling down. In short, he ticks all the wrong boxes. Vespasien's opinion of me isn't much higher.'

'Oh?'

'Painting and music — for him, they're not proper jobs.' Kai strummed a chord, turned one of the tuning pegs, his attention as much on his guitar as on what he was saying. 'He's an old-style deeply conservative rural Frenchman. Conservative with a small C. There's nothing political about it. For him, it's the land — working the land, conserving it — that's what counts.'

'He's certainly passionate about his wines.'

'And he'd do anything for my mother. That's a big plus.' His fingers fell across the guitar strings in a sudden discord. 'But if he ever finds out about Cameron's . . .' He stopped.

'Lady friend in Paris?' Grace supplied.

He shot her a sharp look.

'How did you know?'

'The way you looked at your mother when he said it. Oddly.'

He smiled.

'As simple as that. You're a perceptive woman, you know.'

His eyes didn't leave hers, and she felt herself colour. She could hardly explain that if she'd happened to notice the look he'd sent Angela it was simply because he constantly drew her gaze.

'You're starting to thaw,' she said, speaking to fill the silence. 'You're not so grumpy now.'

He shrugged.

'This place is working its magic. I've turned my phone off. No-one from the outside world knows I'm here. Peace and quiet — for the time being.' His voice took on a harder edge. 'It won't last, though.'

A shadow seemed to cross his face, a reminder of the weariness that had been so much in evidence the day before, and her heart twisted with compassion for him.

'Do you want to talk about it?' she offered quietly, closing the programme on the laptop.

He didn't answer straight away.

'Yes. I'd like that,' he finally said. He paused, clearly gathering his thoughts. 'You know, it was brilliant when I started — and for a long time afterwards. It was eleven years ago, I was seventeen, when I won that TV talent show . . .'

'I voted for you,' Grace said with a laugh. Leaning back against the small table, she was conscious of the smile that hovered over her face, and knew she was happy simply to be listening and watching him.

He laughed.

'Why, thank you for being one of my earliest fans. Yes, it was great at the beginning. I received a big cheque and signed a deal with a record label, my debut album was an immediate hit, and it's been the same with all the albums that followed, one a year on average.

'I'm writing and recording my own songs, I'm touring all over the world, my fans adore me. What's not to like?'

'It sounds wonderful,' Grace murmured, 'but I can imagine some of the downsides. Gruelling schedules, a growing tiredness, adulation that goes to your head . . .'

'That's it. It all becomes unreal. Your plane lands and your manager tells you you're in Tokyo or Sydney. But you could be anywhere. And the tiredness builds and builds. After a while my mind goes numb, I can't write my music any more.' His eyes looked inward, his smile was bleak. 'I become nothing more than a moneymaking machine.'

He fell silent, and Grace didn't speak.

'So the question is, where do I go from here?' he continued some moments later, looking down at his guitar, idly strumming a few chords.

'My manager and I don't see eye to eye about the direction I should take next. Music is my life. I can't stop writing songs and singing them. But touring?

That's a different matter. I've been touring for eleven years. More than a decade. Do I really want to be doing it for ten years more?'

He looked up, his eyes meeting hers.

'My manager and I have had our disagreements over recent months. Things came to a head on Thursday, at the concert in Amsterdam. We had a big row, I walked out — and here I am.' He came to a halt, gaze moving over her features, and smiled, a disarming smile that would melt the iciest heart.

'Thank you, Grace, for listening,' he said softly, 'and for understanding.'

'Thank you for trusting me,' she said, flustered, aware her cheeks were growing warm again. 'But now, I'd, uh, better check the amplifier's working.' She turned to pick up the long, trailing flex. The plug was a French one, two pin, no earth, and it wasn't in good condition.

Even as she pushed the plug into the socket, a warning bell was ringing in her head. Too late.

She yelped as goodness knew how

many volts of electricity thudded through her. The shock threw her backwards. The back of her head hit the floor with a crack.

Underneath the Stars

Perhaps Grace lost consciousness for a second or two. She didn't know. One moment Kai was sitting in the chair strumming his guitar. The next, the guitar dropped to the floor with a clatter and he was up and over to where she lay.

He knelt on one knee beside her, like a sprinter preparing to run.

'Don't move. Don't try to get up.' There was urgency in his voice, fear in his eyes.

'But I . . .'

She heard the noise of feet as people came running, the scrape as both screens were pushed aside. Voices, frightened, distraught, came at her in a rush of questions.

'What's wrong? What's happening?'

'Grace!' Her sister's voice, harsh with concern. 'Tell me you're all right.'

Kai looked up, beyond her.

'Cam, call one-five. Get an ambulance here. Emergency. Quick. Séverine . . .'

And he broke into rapid French.

'I can get up, Kai,' Grace protested, and tried to lift herself on to one elbow. 'I'm fine.'

'Grace, please, just do as I say.' His tone was gentle, as were the hands that pushed her back down to the floor. 'You've had an electric shock. Let's get you to hospital, double-check you're OK.'

How she ached. As if a runaway train had thundered across every bone in her body. When Kai draped her in the blanket Séverine handed him, tucking it in snugly round her neck and shoulders, she couldn't help but surrender to its soft warmth, secure in the knowledge she was safe in his hands. Perfectly safe.

★ ★ ★

'Where am I?' Grace said to no-one in particular when she opened her eyes. Plain painted walls, lime green alternating with beige. No pictures, no paintings.

'In one of the rooms in the emergency

96

department of the hospital.'

Kai! His gravelly voice brought her to full alert.

'What are you doing here?' Never in her wildest dreams could she have imagined herself lying in a hospital bed with singer-songwriter legend Kai Curtis at her side.

She was propped up by pillows and wearing a sleeveless hospital gown over, yes, all her clothes apart from her sweater. Had Kai seen her when they took it off, she wondered, cheeks growing warm at the thought. The blood pressure cuff round her upper arm tightened, and a machine somewhere behind her beeped.

'I came in with you,' Kai said. His hair was mussed up, as if he'd been constantly pushing his fingers through it. 'I followed the ambulance. Your sister wanted to come, too, but I said no.'

Grace smiled.

'The show must go on.'

The concern in his eyes eased.

'Exactly.'

She saw him hesitate before he spoke.

'Grace.' He took her hands in both his, and she didn't question it, loving the warmth and strength they imparted. 'For one horrible moment back there, I thought you were dead. You weren't, thank God, but I still feel responsible.'

'Don't be ridiculous, Kai. How . . . ?'

'It was my amplifier. You can't imagine how I feel about that.'

'Look, if we're shouldering responsibilities, I should shoulder my fair share. The plug was moving — just a little — at the end of the flex. The wires must have been loose, and the plug looked a bit battered. I should never have plugged it in.'

'That's what I don't get. My equipment is always in good condition. My manager sees to that.'

Grace shrugged.

'Well, who knows? But I'd already sensed something wasn't quite right. I'd half taken my fingers off the plug.'

From the corridor outside came the sound of footsteps approaching. Kai gave her hands a gentle squeeze before letting them slide from his grip, slowly, as if reluctantly.

'I'll take you back to the château when the doctors give you the all-clear,' he said, standing up. 'Is that OK with you?'

She could only nod. It occurred to her that he'd said he would say hello and goodbye to his brother, then leave, and she now wondered why he hadn't. All of a sudden her heart was full to bursting. She watched his broad back as he walked out the door and found herself wishing she could call him back.

But how could she?

His concern for her was genuine, she didn't doubt it. Of course he'd been worried. Everyone had. There'd been nothing special about the way he'd accompanied her to the hospital and stayed with her, though. Anyone else would have done the same, wouldn't they? She mustn't read too much into his actions.

Even so, she was in danger of falling in love with him. She recognised it now. While he, of course, would never feel the same way about her.

★ ★ ★

'Even if I were a world-famous artist . . .' Cameron began. Hand cupping Grace's elbow as he steered her across the grand salon, he leaned close, his words for her ears only. 'Which I'm not — yet,' he added with a laugh. 'I still wouldn't have to spend my time dodging photographers. Not like Kai.'

There was envy, and a hint of petulance, in his tone. But Grace heard relief too. Though jealous of his brother's fame, he almost certainly welcomed his own anonymity.

'Let's sit here, shall we?' Grace said, stopping at a two-seater sofa midway along the catwalk. It was two o'clock. Music played in the background, people chatted and greeted old friends, the fashion show was due to start and there was a definite buzz of excitement in the air.

'Perfect,' Cameron said.

The doctors had given Grace the all-clear. Her heart rhythm was normal, the shock hadn't caused any burns, she'd broken no bones when she was thrown back on to the floor. Kai had brought her back to the château, driving past the cars that were already lining up in the front and straight into the barn where the family's vehicles were housed.

'I'd like to stay with you for the fashion show,' he'd said, and her heart had leaped at his words, 'but if I do,' he went on, 'before the week is out your picture will be on the front page of all the tabloids. And you won't want that, believe me.'

So he'd asked his brother to sit with her, and part of her — a very small part — was happy about the arrangement. Cameron knew everyone, it seemed, and delighted in bringing her up to speed on all the gossip.

'See the woman with my mother? The ex-president's wife,' he now said. 'A real coup for my mama, getting her here.'

Moments later he leaned forward conspiratorially.

'See that man over there? The one

with the camera? He's with 'La Mode de Demain', the fashion mag. Looks like your sister's going to get good coverage.'

Then he nudged her again.

'Uh-oh. That woman with my brother?' Grace watched Kai come into the grand salon, accompanied — or perhaps pursued — by a young woman half-turned towards him, matching his every step. 'She works for 'Bonjour!', the gossip mag. So now they'll all know where he is. He made the right call, keeping you away from him.'

Grace bit her lip, heart heavy as she caught this glimpse of the lack of privacy, the hounding he must endure on a daily basis. He made his way across the room, stopping frequently to say a few words here, clasp a hand or shoulder there, and his smile reminded her of a politician meeting and greeting out of duty, not pleasure.

He glanced across at her, and she thought there was genuine warmth in the smile he sent her before taking a seat at the far end, next to Barbs.

Natasha was nowhere in sight. Doubtless she was in the side room, checking the models' clothes before they came out on to the catwalk. One of Pierre's grandchildren, Cameron had told her, was a DJ at weekends, and had been put in charge of the music. There was no sign of Vespasien or Johnno.

'They're in the wine cellars,' Cameron said. 'Where else?'

News of Grace's accident with the plug had clearly done the rounds, and she was moved when people she knew, and others she didn't, came up to her to wish her well, glad to see she was fully recovered, that no harm had been done.

Angela was in her element. She'd changed into a floaty dress with a handkerchief hem, its vibrant cherry red both clashing with and complementing her orange hair and nails and the long shocking pink scarf she'd tied bandana-style across her forehead.

She thanked everyone for attending, making sure to include a famous star of stage and screen, the ex-president's wife, and a highly regarded poet in her thanks. Grace couldn't help smiling at her snobbery. Deliberate or unconscious, it was harmless and rather endearing.

The music swelled, the models walked out on to the catwalk — simply a long narrow space between the chairs — and the show was underway.

Angela gave a brief commentary of each outfit while Marie-Laure translated into French. The models strode up and down the catwalk, tossing back their hair, putting hands to hips, striking a pose like true professionals.

The clothes were fabulous, and the audience oohed and clapped their enthusiasm. Grace could see almost immediately that the show was going to be a huge success, and she was filled with pride for her talented sister.

At last the music came to an end, the three models stayed on the catwalk, the audience clapped and clapped and Angela darted into the side room. When she reappeared seconds later pulling a broadly smiling Natasha out behind her, the clapping rose to a crescendo.

'Thank you, thank you,' Natasha said over and over again. 'Thank you so much for your support and enthusiasm.' She spoke in breathless gulps as if she'd just run a marathon. 'It's greatly appreciated, believe me. If any of you would like to come backstage . . .' she gestured towards the side room '. . . to look at the clothes in greater detail, please don't hesitate. But first . . .' She paused with the dramatic pause of someone about to make a big announcement. 'First, Kai Curtis is going to sing for us.'

A buzz of voices, quick movements of heads as people turned to speak to their neighbours. The excitement was tangible, the hush instant when Kai got to his feet, guitar in hand.

Grace's heart jolted into a fast, insistent beat. She'd seen him sing in videos on the internet, of course. She'd never seen him perform live.

The grand salon was a large room, but there was something very intimate about performing there, she thought as she listened to his first song. Something closeup and personal that you wouldn't get in a vast stadium, or by watching a video.

He stood leaning close to the microphone, and she watched his fingers move over the strings and frets of the guitar, watched his lips as he sang the words of his song, and she recalled with a pang the way those fingers, warm and strong, had held hers, and how those lips — just once — had touched hers in the lightest of kisses.

He sang a selection of his hits, all-time favourites with a fast, rhythmic beat that had his audience tapping their feet or clapping in time or singing along, while others were slow, lyrical numbers whose raw emotion brought a painful lump to Grace's throat.

'Wow, that was something special,' she breathed when Kai took his final bow. It almost hurt to speak, so moved was she by the sheer power of his performance.

'He's good, isn't he?' Cameron said, hand at her elbow as she stood up. 'Come on. Let's circulate.'

Grace looked along to the far end of the catwalk. The star of stage and screen had draped herself around Kai. Congratulating him on a brilliant performance, no doubt. The woman from 'Bonjour!' hovered close behind. She and Kai lived in different worlds, Grace thought, conscious of a bitter realisation. His was a world of fame, success and beautiful people. How could she compete with that?

She brought a smile to her face.

'Let's go and congratulate my sister, Cam.'

'I'm just so relieved,' Natasha said when first Grace then Cameron wrapped her in a heartfelt hug. 'People are ordering my clothes in their droves.'

Natasha's cheeks were pink, her eyes held tears, a huge smile filled her face, and Grace squeezed her hands, sharing her happiness.

'You were fantastic, Nat. Well done!'

Sévérine and her group of helpers brought round dishes of nibbles and glasses of Château Beauvallon red and white. Angela, as flushed with the success of the event as Natasha, moved from one small group to another, clearly loving every moment of the afternoon.

Barbs was chatting to Marie-Laure and the models. Johnno, looking rather unsteady on his feet, together with Vespasien, had finally put in an appearance. They stood in one corner, nursing a glass of red each. Loki lay stretched out between them.

Grace stayed with Cameron. Like Angela, they moved from group to group, talking about Natasha and her clothes — and, inevitably, about Kai's performance.

It was a special kind of torture, she thought, to be reminded so often about the man. Every time someone spoke about him, she couldn't help looking his way, and every single time, she found, he was surrounded by women, deep in conversation with them.

As the afternoon progressed and night fell, people took their leave, driving off in their twos and threes, until only the family and their house guests were left. Pierre brought in a tray holding two bottles and eight long-stemmed glasses which he placed on a table by the wall.

'A glass of pétillant each, I think,' Vespasien said, taking one of the bottles and twisting undone the metal wire round its top.

Grace, along with the others, crossed towards the table and their host. Where was Kai, she was wondering, when her hand was clasped by someone behind her. She turned, and pleasure whispered across her skin. Kai.

'Do you want some bubbly?'

She shook her head.

'Then come with me.' Already, he was drawing her with him, across and out of the room. His hand round hers was warm, assured.

'Where are we going?' she asked, breathless, caught up in the adventure of it.

'Up to the second floor. You'll need your jacket. We can access the tower from there.'

'The tower? Oh!' She recalled the circular tower as high as the roof ridge that stood at one corner of the château.

Kai snatched up his coat from a chair, hooked it over his shoulder, and they ran side by side up the stairs, past the first floor and on to the second. He waited while she ran along to her room to fetch her jacket.

Seconds later, she was back, zipping it up as she went. Kai, she saw, had put his long leather coat on, pulling the collar up around his ears.

'This way,' he said, taking her hand again.

He led her along the corridor. No time to stop to look at the paintings that lined the walls. Grace's pulse was racing. She knew where he was taking her, didn't know what he had in mind. But she trusted him totally, she realised. Despite his reputation with women, she somehow knew he meant her no harm.

They came to a low door dark with age and studded with nail heads. Kai pressed down on the latch and pushed it open, reaching inside to click on a light switch. Cold air and the earthy smell of stone met Grace's nostrils. In the yellow light of an unshaded bulb, she could see wide steps twisting both upwards and down.

'Go up,' Kai said. 'And hold on to the rope.'

Grace seized the thick, rough rope secured at intervals to the curving wall and climbed. She could hear Kai coming up behind her. Over the centuries, the stairs, carved from the soft creamy-white local stone, had been hollowed out in the middle by the passage of many feet. There were only ten of them and they ended in another door. Kai reached past her to push it open, and freezing outside air hit her face.

'Go on,' he said.

Grace looked around her as she stepped through the doorway — and gasped. What a beautiful surprise. She stood on a circular platform open to the elements, the tower's flat roof, she supposed. A chest-high wall ran all the way round.

The moon hadn't yet risen, but there were stars in their millions, sparkling, twinkling against the velvet blackness of the cloud-free sky.

'Oh, Kai,' she said, breath catching. Standing beside her, he too was looking out. 'Living where I do, I've never seen so many stars. Look,' she said, 'there's Orion, the hunter.'

'And look — there — the Plough.'

'Where?'

He put his arm round her shoulder, drawing her close so she could look along the line of his other arm into the night sky.

'Can you see it? Like a scoop with a long handle. Follow the front edge and you'll come to the pole star. True north.'

And somehow she wasn't looking at the stars any more. Breathlessness of a different kind had her in its grip, and she was twisting round within the circle of his arms, looking at Kai instead.

His face was a paler shadow against

the dark of his hair and coat. She breathed in the scents of him — leather and cologne — and the woodsmoke that drifted through the still air.

For a long moment neither moved. Then, with a swiftly murmured 'Grace', he placed his hands at her waist, pulling her against the length of his body, and she'd brought her hands up to his face, running her fingertips across his beard-roughened jaw, pushing them up into his hair.

And she closed her eyes when his lips came down on hers in a kiss that sent waves of sensation pulsing through her body.

Fire in His Kiss

When at last they drew apart, it was as if she'd lost some part of herself, Grace thought, and a tiny chill of warning shivered down her spine.

She made no protest, though, when he pressed her head against his shoulder, and wrapped his arms around her, holding her tightly to him. There'd be no harm if he held her a little longer, would there? It seemed so right.

'I've been wanting to do that all day,' he said, brushing the pad of his thumb up across her cheek, 'ever since that dreadful accident.'

'Kissing it better?' she murmured.

She sensed him smile.

'And have I? No headaches? Pain? No after-effects?'

Hmm, she thought, body still a-tremble from his kiss. Definite after-effects, but not from the electric shock.

'I'm fine, Kai. Really. I got off lightly.'

'Good. I'm glad.' His arms tightened

round her in a brief hug.

'And I understand totally why you couldn't kiss me before,' she said, reaching up, fingers of one hand twisting in the hair at the back of his head.

'I have to be so careful what I do in public. That sounds self-pitying. It's not meant to be.'

'I know.' With sadness in her heart, she recalled how insistent he'd been that she shouldn't be seen in his company during the fashion show. At the hospital too he'd been distant, for fear perhaps that one of the staff would take photos and sell them to the tabloids. 'You have to behave with decorum at all times. Like a politician.'

'Or the royals.'

Grace laughed.

'Now you're sounding smug.'

Kai laughed, too, and they fell silent, at ease, Grace sensed, in each other's company. From below, far off, came the bark of a fox, and nearer the château the unearthly hoo-hoo of a tawny owl. Snow-covered hills rose to the south, ghostly white against the black of the sky.

'It's wonderful out here,' Grace said into his shoulder. 'Timeless. Beautiful. Thank you so much for showing it me.'

'We're above the world. Away from it all.'

'We'll have to re-join it soon.' Regret was heavy in her voice. 'It must be almost time for dinner.'

'You're right. But before we go . . .'

Grace lifted her head, frowning at the sudden switch in his tone, now grave yet oddly hesitant.

'What is it?'

He cupped her face in both hands, tilting it up towards him.

'I want you to take care, Grace. There's something going on here at the château. Something's not quite right.' His words, quiet, earnestly spoken, carried the weight of conviction.

'I don't understand.'

'My equipment's always good quality stuff, and well looked after. You should never have got an electric shock. You could have been killed.'

'It could have been you. You could have been the one to put the plug in the socket.'

'True. But it was you who flagged up the problem with the painting.'

'The painting?' she echoed. 'The Sisley? It's gone. It's not hanging on the wall any more.'

'I know. I went back, saw it wasn't there.'

'So did I.' And as she spoke, she felt a coldness in her veins that had nothing to do with the freezing night air. Her first instinct was denial. Kai was being melodramatic, overly protective. She was surely in no danger. But perhaps he was right. There had been two incidents, two occurrences that were hard to explain.

'You think the two things are connected?'

'I don't know. But I aim to find out.' There was no disguising the steel of determination in his voice.

'There has to be a simple, rational explanation. For starters, we can ask Angela about the painting — she was the one who sent it off to be restored. She should know where it is now.'

'And I've left a message with my manager, asking him what he can tell me about the amplifier. No reply as yet. But I meant what I said — I can't always be with you, Grace. You must be watchful, alert.' And he pulled her towards him, gently, and pressed a kiss to her mouth, a soft tender kiss that left her aching for more.

* * *

'Wasn't it just brilliant, darlings?'

Grace couldn't help smiling as Angela returned yet again to her theme. She glanced across at Kai who sat opposite her, and felt warmth steal over her when he smiled back.

He'd left her at the door to her room on the second floor before heading for the main staircase and the floor below. In her room she'd had a quick shower and changed into a simply styled zinging yellow dress, another of Natasha's creations. Her sister was nowhere to be seen. She'd already gone down to dinner, Grace supposed.

And so it turned out. Grace had run down the stairs and along to the dining-room to find Kai waiting for her by the door. The others were already seated or in the process of sitting down.

'You look wonderful,' Kai murmured as he escorted her to her seat, earning an archly raised eyebrow from Cameron, in the chair next to hers, that brought stinging colour to her cheeks.

'The ex-president's wife was a darling, wasn't she?' Angela was saying to the table at large. 'A positive darling.'

'She's ordered three dresses and a skirt,' Natasha said. Her sister was almost bubbling over with happiness, Grace thought, and was immensely pleased for her.

'You've worked very hard, Natasha dear,' Barbs said. 'You deserve every bit of your success.'

The starter, scallops in a delicate sauce, was brought in. The room was warm, and filled with the scents of pine, orange zest and cloves from the tree in the corner.

Vespasien, seated as usual at the head of the table, peeled the foil off the top of a bottle of wine.

Cameron leaned in close to Grace.

'So what kept you and Kai away from the dinner table? You missed apéritifs.'

Vespasien pulled the cork out of the bottle with a pop.

'I think you'll all enjoy this one.'

Cameron's glance flicked from Grace to Kai and back to her. She felt herself colour again, and turned away, towards Vespasien.

'The 2005 vintage?'

A moment's hesitation, swiftly followed by a gracious smile.

'As good in its way,' he said. 'Two thousand and thirteen. An interesting year. Here, try some,' and he took her glass and half-filled it. 'Remember — inhale — and chew.'

Grace laughed and did as she was told.

'Hmm, that's lovely,' she said a

short while later. 'Smooth summer fruit — tangy and delicious.'

'Got some for me?' Johnno said, holding out his glass.

'Angela . . .' Kai said. His mother sat at the foot of the long rectangular table, at the opposite end to her husband. 'That painting Grace was a bit puzzled by — I couldn't help noticing it wasn't there any more.'

Vespasien, in the middle of pouring Johnno his wine, looked up sharply.

'Which painting?'

Angela paused before replying, and when she spoke there was reluctance in her voice.

'The Sisley, darling. Chestnut trees along a country lane.'

'So where is it?' He looked at Grace. 'Puzzled? How can anyone be puzzled by a Sisley?'

'It's been restored,' she said, 'but rather clumsily in places.' Vespasien made an impatient circling movement with his hand, indicating she should go on. She drew in a breath and told him what she'd recounted to Kai.

He heard her out.

'This is your job?' he then said. 'You know about these things. Correct?'

She nodded. He looked down the length of the table at his wife.

'It's a valuable painting. I don't recall being asked if I wanted it restored.'

Loki, alerted perhaps by the coldness in his master's voice, looked up from the floor and gave a low growl. Cameron shifted in his chair. Grace bit her lip and looked at Kai. The conversation, already uncomfortable, risked turning into a full-scale domestic row.

'That's something,' Kai said, 'that should be discussed later perhaps.'

Vespasien held his stance a moment longer before sinking back into his chair, one hand dropping to the floor to tangle in Loki's fur.

'D'accord,' he said at last to his stepson. 'But let me get this straight,' he continued, eyes on his wife again. 'You sent the painting away to be restored. It's been restored — badly. It's come

122

back. And now it's disappeared. Have I got that right?'

'Uh, maybe I can help with that,' Cameron said, to Grace's surprise. 'I took it up to my studio. I wanted to study it, and the light's much better there.'

Vespasien turned his cold gaze on his younger stepson.

'Put it back where it belongs. Although it's always useful, I suppose, to study a talented artist.'

The slight emphasis on the word 'talented' brought a flush to Cameron's face, and Grace knew to her dismay that Vespasien's barb had found its mark.

'Hey,' she said faux-brightly, 'you promised to show me your studio, Cameron. I'd love to see your paintings.'

'Yes, me too,' Natasha added.

'And me,' Barbs chimed in.

And all of a sudden, everyone was talking, tucking into their starter, relieved that the awkward moment was over.

Everyone except Kai. Scraping back his chair, he stood up and moved down the table to his mother, bending low to squeeze her shoulders and murmur in her ear.

An apology, perhaps, for raising the subject, Grace thought, touched by this private moment between mother and son, and reassured when Angela squeezed her son's hand in return and he went back to his seat.

They talked about all sorts, reliving — yet again — the success of the fashion show, discussing wines, firming up plans for the next day.

'Our murder mystery dinner tomorrow evening, darlings. Possibly the start of a brand-new business venture for me so it's important it goes well. Nineteen-twenties costumes, remember,' Angela cautioned. 'It'll be great fun. Won't it, Vespi darling?' she said, beaming a smile at her husband.

He raised his glass to her.

'I'm looking forward to it.' Sitting back in his chair, with his Irish setter stretched out on the floor beside him, he looked relaxed and content. Marital harmony had been restored, Grace sensed.

After a long, rambling but surprisingly funny story about a disaster at an auction, Johnno stood up.

'I'm off outside for a ciggie. Anyone care to join me?'

No-one did, but Angela stood up.

'I need to check on the main course. I'll come with you.'

'He's giving up on the first of January,' Barbs said. 'He says the same thing every year,' she added drily.

And that, of course, led to a discussion of New Year's resolutions.

'I intend going to Florence, to the Uffizi Gallery, for a week at least,' Grace said, 'so I can spend as much time as I want studying the paintings.'

'That's a wish list, not a resolution,' Natasha protested.

'You've never been to Florence?' Kai asked, a smile in his eyes.

'Just one day. It was terribly rushed. Not long enough.'

'I'm going to lose a few kilos,' Barbs said.

'And I'm going to make big changes

in my life,' Cameron announced.

'About time too,' Vespasien muttered.

It occurred to Grace that Kai had remained silent about any plans or resolutions he might have made for the future. Knowing he'd come to the château to get away from his ordinary life — extraordinary life, rather — she didn't bring the matter up. Neither did anyone else, she noticed.

Johnno returned, and Angela, Séverine and another woman carried the main course in — a gigot of lamb that filled the room with its aroma, together with a selection of winter vegetables.

'And we have some very British mint sauce to go with the lamb.' Angela laughed.

The main course was a great success, as was the next, tangy cheeses served with dressed salad leaves and crusty, yeasty home-baked bread. The wine Vespasien poured for each course was excellent, and the conversation lively and wide-ranging, all awkwardness over the Sisley just a memory.

Grace talked and smiled and laughed, and more often than she could count, her eyes met Kai's across the table in long moments of shared warmth.

The last course was a café gourmand, coffee served with a selection of mini-desserts.

Vespasien dropped a sugar cube into his cup and looked down along the table at his wife.

'Where did you send it? The Sisley. Who did you get to restore it?'

Grace tensed as the table fell silent. She sensed Cameron, beside her, stiffen. Kai looked grim. Vespasien was worrying at the subject like a dog at a bone, refusing to let it go. But was that so surprising? He'd had to be single-minded to run his thriving wine business and keep the château and grounds in good order.

'Ah.' To Grace's surprise, it was Johnno who spoke. He cleared his throat. 'Confession time, Vesp. It was a friend of mine.'

He stopped, and Vespasien frowned.

'So what's his name?'

127

'That's just it.' Johnno's tone was apologetic. 'I've been racking my brains ever since you asked about the painting. I can't remember.'

'Not a good friend, then?'

'More of an acquaintance really.'

Vespasien stirred his coffee thoughtfully, put his spoon down, and all the time his eyes never left Johnno.

'Why that painting? Why not one of the others?'

Kai moved restlessly.

'Let's drop it for now, shall we?' His voice was a growl.

Vespasien turned his gaze on his stepson. For the space of several seconds he seemed to be debating whether to pursue the matter.

'Very well,' he said at last, and it was as if everyone else expelled a collective breath.

It had been a good question, though, Grace thought. One she'd love to know the answer to.

* * *

'Kai kissed me. Did he kiss you? Yesterday, I mean,' Grace said, sitting down on her sister's bed, tucking her legs beneath her.

'Ah, now, that'd be telling.'

'For goodness' sake. Don't be so irritating, Natasha. Tell me. Did he?'

It was a couple of hours later, and Natasha was already in bed. Grace, not sure she could fall asleep straight away, had come to join her.

'No. He didn't,' her sister admitted, and Grace felt the tension ease from her shoulders. She didn't know why her sister's answer should matter so much, but it did.

'Oh Grace . . .' Natasha was pushing herself upright, concern on her face. 'You've fallen for him, haven't you?'

She nodded.

'I rather think I have.'

'Grace, love . . .' Her sister took both hands in hers. 'You've got to take care. I don't want to see you hurt.'

'I had a look online. He's had two long-term relationships. Some short-lived ones

too, of course. So you never know . . .'
Her chin tilted, and she braved a smile. 'I
could be the third long-term one.'

'Grace . . .' Natasha's arms went round
her, pulling her into a hug. She stroked
her hair. 'Let's hope you are. But . . .'

'I know, I know. Pie in the sky.' Grace
was glad her sister couldn't see her face
and the tears that filled her eyes. 'At
best, Kai and I will be together for the
few days we're both here at the château.
And then — and then we'll go our sepa-
rate ways.'

It didn't bear thinking about. But she
had to face reality. Kai could have his
pick of beautiful, interesting women.
Why would he choose her? She drew
away from her sister and cuffed the tears
from her cheeks.

Natasha took hold of her hands again.
Her eyes were bright with curiosity.

'So what was it like, his kiss?'

Grace's mind flashed back to those
long moments at the top of the tower,
high above the world. She recalled the
warmth and strength of his arms around

her, the intensity of his lips on hers, and her whole being was suffused with a warm glow. She smiled.

'It set me on fire,' she said simply.

Special Someone

The following morning, Grace waited until Natasha had finished getting ready. That way, they could go downstairs to breakfast together. Safety in numbers, she reasoned.

She'd been inclined to dismiss Kai's conviction that something was not quite right at the château, his warning to her to take care and be on the alert. Imagining she was in some kind of danger had all seemed just too far-fetched. But now, after a restless night, she was more ready to give him credence.

She'd slept badly, reliving the events of the day before. The thud as electricity jolted through her body, throwing her backwards, had occurred and recurred in her dreams, over and over, in an endless loop.

Over and over, too, were a terse exchange between Cameron and his stepfather and a face-off between Kai and Vespasien, taut and tense, two stags prepared to lock antlers in the crash of battle.

And most pervasive of all, still achingly vivid in her mind even now she was awake, the dream of herself in Kai's arms, as the two of them shared a passionate embrace.

She couldn't stop thinking about him. She slowed as she and Natasha reached the first-floor landing. Maybe she could be looking — casually — at one of the paintings just as Kai came along, heading down for breakfast.

'Grace!' Her sister's voice held a warning. 'It won't work, Grace.'

Grace laughed.

'I didn't realise I was so transparent.' Anyway, she thought, as delicious aromas of baking and coffee drifted up towards her, maybe he was already in the kitchen having his breakfast, and she hastened her pace down the stairs.

Arriving first at the kitchen, a few metres in front of her sister, she pushed open the door. He wasn't there, and she felt a twist of disappointment.

Sévérine was at the oven. Wearing oven gloves, she'd pulled a tray of croissants out and was lifting one up to check its underside.

Angela and Cameron stood over by the door that led to the barn. They stopped talking, abruptly, heads turning to the door to see who had come in, and it seemed to Grace they both had to make a deliberate effort to shake themselves out of the conversation they'd been having. A serious one, clearly, judging by the expression she'd glimpsed on their faces.

'I'm sorry. I should have knocked.'

'Grace, darling — no need to apologise.' Angela beamed a bright smile. 'And Natasha. Did you sleep well? Hungry? Come on in, darlings.'

With a bustle of movement and a scraping of chairs across tiles, the four of them sat down — and Grace gasped in shock as two hands, warm and strong, hands she'd dreamed about, gripped her upper arms. Kai. She had her back to the door, hadn't heard him come in. Twisting round to look at him, she couldn't prevent the shy smile that spread over her face.

'Hi.'

He smiled back, and his hands stroked down her arms and up again, just once. She could feel their warmth through the thickness of her sweater, and her heart did a crazy flip-flop.

'All right?' he asked.

She nodded, and he sat down beside her, shifting his chair so close that his shoulder brushed against hers.

'Vespi's already had his breakfast,' Angela was saying. 'Barbs and Johnno will be down shortly, I expect.' She was looking with interest at the two of them. Cameron had a knowing smile on his face. There was concern in Natasha's eyes, though.

Yes, Grace thought. There was danger here. Her sister was right to be concerned. Grace was in danger of losing her heart — to a man who was way out of her league.

'Hey, Grace,' Cameron said, breaking into her thoughts. 'What do you say to coming up to the studio this morning, having a look at my work?'

Was that what he'd been discussing so earnestly, so anxiously, with his mother as she came into the kitchen? Grace gave herself a mental shake. Surely not.

'Thanks. That'd be great. I'd love to.'

'What's everyone else planning for this morning?' Kai asked, and Grace felt herself tense, sensing he wasn't simply making small talk.

'It would be really fabulous, darlings,' Angela said, 'if all four of you could spend the morning in the studio. Till eleven? Twelve? How does that sound?'

'Fine by me,' Kai said.

'Me too,' Natasha agreed. 'After yesterday I just want to chill. I don't mind where.'

'Perfect,' Angela said with a laugh. 'Vespi and I are going to be planting the clues for the murder mystery dinner and, of course, we don't want you to see where we've hidden them. Barbs and Johnno are being absolute darlings, too. They've promised to stay in their suite until lunchtime at least.'

The studio was on the second floor. Cameron pushed open the door, holding it back to let Grace and Natasha go on in before him.

Kai stood beside his brother, guitar and sheets of music in his hands. Grace looked back at him as she entered the studio, and their eyes met. He had a small smile on his face. A smile for her, Grace wondered, pulse fluttering.

The room was large and airy, and cluttered with easels, two sofas arranged at right angles to each other, small tables covered in loose-leaf papers, sketchpads, half-finished drawings, and a huge old-fashioned dresser so tall it almost touched the room's high ceiling.

Pots and jam jars, filled with brushes and charcoals, and trays of paints in tubes covered every available horizontal surface. The familiar smells of oil paint, linseed oil and mineral spirit were strong in Grace's nostrils.

She smiled with delight, her gaze drawn to the windows set high into one wall of the room, and the soft, even light that came through them.

'We're north-facing here, aren't we?' she said, turning to Cameron and adding with a laugh, 'I hope you realise just how lucky you are.'

'Oh, I do. Believe me, I do.'

Kai came to stand beside her, and awareness of his closeness whispered down her spine.

Natasha was sitting on one of the sofas. Legs curled beneath her, pencil in hand, she was flicking through the pages of her sketchpad.

'A nineteenth-century Beauvallon de Mottefort,' Kai said, 'one of Vespasien's distant ancestors, had this room converted into a studio. He was quite a famous artist in his day.' He cast a swift glance round. 'The Sisley isn't here?'

'Uh, no,' Cameron said, clearly flustered by the sudden change of subject. 'I took it back downstairs.'

'That was quick.'

'Yes,' Cameron said with a laugh that

sounded just a little forced. 'My stepfather's wish is my command.'

Grace moved away. Canvasses on the floor were propped against the walls. Others, lots of them, hung on the walls, crammed together in a higgledy-piggledy display. Grace went from one to the next, stooping close to examine them.

Vespasien had been wrong to dismiss his stepson's ability, she decided. And cruel to do so in company. Cameron did have talent. His work was precise and painstaking though still immature, perhaps. He hadn't yet found a style, a vision, he could call his own.

She stopped by a group of just under a dozen sketches, all framed in the same blond wood. The first showed the dome of Montmartre, with the head of a priest in the foreground. Another portrayed a souvenir seller, the Eiffel Tower in the background.

'These are good,' she said, impressed.

Cameron's face broke into a wide smile.

'My Paris places and faces series. I'm

glad you like them.'

'They remind me of Naymar-Ferris's work. The subject matter. The style, too.'

She spoke absently, her attention not fully fixed on what she was looking at. Kai had sat down at one end of the second sofa. Leaning back, the ankle of one leg resting on the knee of the other, he was playing his guitar and singing, quietly, for himself alone. It was a song she'd heard so many times before. A haunting love song, the bittersweet words and melody bringing an ache to her throat.

She saw Cameron hesitate.

'Kai says you know — why I go to Paris so often, I mean.'

'There's someone there,' she said softly. 'Someone special.'

Kai was singing another love song, slow and lilting, one she hadn't heard before, and the ache in her throat swelled with emotion.

'That's right . . .' He stopped, and she had the impression he'd come to a decision. Twisting away, he crouched down beside the tall, ornately carved dresser, pulled open one of its two lower doors and drew something out. He stood up and handed it to her without speaking, and Grace could sense he was holding his breath, waiting for her reaction.

She saw Kai glance up at her and Cameron, then down again at his fingers as they played across the strings of the guitar. Whatever Cameron wanted to show her, it was plain Kai had seen it before.

It was a sketch the same size as the others, and housed in the same blond wood frame. The sketch that completed the series, Grace thought, the one that meant the most, hidden away for obvious reasons.

It showed a man in his thirties, standing in a space whose walls were hung with paintings, a space too large and impersonal to be someone's house. He was almost certainly, Grace surmised, the owner or manager of one of the galleries in Paris where Cameron had shown his work. With the classical perfection of his features and his carefully crafted hair, he reminded her of a statue from antiquity.

'I can see why you fell for him,' she said, and saw the tension go from Cameron's shoulders.

'He means the world to me.'

A heartfelt statement, simply spoken, and the ache in her throat was an ache of longing. How wonderful if she ever meant as much to Kai!

With a sigh she looked away. Cameron had left the door to the dresser ajar, and she caught sight of canvasses propped inside, some wrapped in cloth. She smiled.

'What else have you got in there? Have you done some paintings of him?'

All at once bright colour stained Cameron's cheeks, and he pushed the door closed with his foot.

'No, they're nothing. Just some old rubbish of mine.'

Grace frowned as the noise of a motor, growing steadily louder, drew her attention. The others had heard it too. Kai's fingers had stilled on the strings of his guitar.

It was a rumbling roar, low overhead, very loud now, a sound Grace had heard before but couldn't place. And then she did, and looked at Kai in horror.

A helicopter, circling above the château.

'They've found you,' she said, and her voice shook. No need to say who 'they' were. She could have wept for him.

His expression was grim.

'It had to happen sooner or later. I'm surprised they took so long.'

Natasha looked stricken.

'It's my fault. If I hadn't had the fashion show here . . . I'm so sorry.'

'Don't cut yourself up about it,' Kai said. 'I've had two days of freedom. I've done well.'

Two days. Grace's heart was heavy.

'If it's any consolation,' she said, 'they can't land. With all this snow, they won't be able to see where they're landing.'

Natasha rolled her eyes.

'Good old Grace. Practical as ever.'

'There's a calmness about you,' Kai

said, 'an inner calm that helps me see things more clearly.'

★ ★ ★

They'd reached the treeline, and he put his arm round her shoulders, drawing her to him with that easy familiarity she found so beguiling. He'd waited deliberately, she knew, until they entered the forest. Surrounded by trees, there was less risk of being seen.

'You must have been like that right from the start,' he went on. 'That's why your parents gave you the name they did.'

She laughed, her breath forming a cloud in the cold air.

''Fraid not. By all accounts I came kicking and screaming into this world.'

He laughed. She leaned her head against his shoulder, and they walked on along the woodland path, their feet crunching into the snow.

It was late afternoon and the light was beginning to fade. Grace breathed in the scents of peat and mushrooms, from time to time picking up the rustle as a small hidden creature — her squirrel, perhaps? — moved through the under-growth.

She was happy, and hoped Kai was, too. The moments when his privacy was guaranteed, when he could be himself, had to be rare indeed, she thought sadly.

The helicopter had circled the château and gone away again. Shortly afterwards, the landline had begun ringing, over and over, prompting Kai to issue a statement via his manager saying he was spending a quiet Christmas with his family and asking for his privacy to be respected.

Almost all newspapers and maga-zines would comply, he explained. But it wouldn't stop the paparazzi, for ever on the hunt for the exclusive photo.

Pierre, the aged retainer, had come in during lunch to report that there was indeed a group of photographers stand-ing outside the gatehouse, and that his son had caught two of them trying to climb over the high stone wall that ran all round the château park.

'They'll have cameras with telephoto lenses,' Angela said. 'Do be careful, Kai darling.'

Another reason to stay inside, and that had been fine. After a snack lunch — a tasty croque-monsieur each — the four of them had helped with preparations for the evening's murder mystery dinner.

'There'll be twenty-four of us altogether,' Angela said. 'It'll be fabulous.'

Vespasien had said nothing, but his mouth tightened into a thin line, and Grace had the uncomfortable impression he'd been totting up the cost.

But he'd smiled and nodded his approval later in the afternoon when he saw Cameron and Natasha shoulder to shoulder in the dining room, one straightening the cutlery and the other the glasses.

'Hmm,' he murmured, 'the lady in Paris had better watch out. She might be about to lose him.'

Grace smiled at the memory. Vespasien couldn't have been more wrong, though it was up to Cameron to put him right, of course. All in all, the afternoon had been great fun. They'd worked hard and laughed a lot.

Kai, out of concern for her safety, she supposed, had stayed with her the whole time. And who could complain about that?

'You don't need to stay with me all the time,' she now said, wondering even as she spoke how she could be so foolish, wishing him away from her when he was like a fever in her blood, a drug she could hardly bear to do without.

'I'm really not convinced there's anything going on at the château. And the thing with the plug — it was an accident, Kai, surely. Faulty wiring.'

He shook his head.

'I'm playing it safe. Until I find out what's going on I want you to be with me or your sister or in your room with the door locked. No wandering off alone. Just in case.' He paused.

'Maybe I stay with you because I want to,' he added quietly, and her heart stood still for an instant.

They walked on in an easy silence broken only by the crunch of their feet on the snow and the cawing of rooks high in the trees. Kai's arm was a warm, welcome weight across her shoulders.

'Hey.' There was a smile in his voice as he slowed to a halt and pointed down at the ground. 'Do you see that?'

They'd stopped where another path cut across the one they were on, and it looked as if someone had been digging, randomly, turning over large clods of earth here and there, the dark soil and mulching leaves a vivid contrast to the white of the snow.

'Wild boar,' he said. 'Rooting around for food.'

'Let's hope they found some. It can't be easy, in the middle of winter.'

He laughed.

'Your sister's right, you know. There's a very practical side to you.' He drew her round to face him, and Grace was conscious of his hands at her waist and, when he spoke, of a subtle change in tone and expression. 'I like that. Very much,' he said softly.

'Oh.' All at once, she felt breathless. Her gaze took in the warmth of his eyes, the smile that curved his mouth, the strong lines of the face she knew so well, and her heart lurched into a fast, insistent beat.

His hands came up to smooth a strand of hair from her face.

'My brother showed you his sketch of the special person in his life.' The pad of his thumb trailed tantalisingly across her lower lip. 'I rather think I've found my special person in you.'

Grace was lost for words. She reached up, fingertips brushing along the rasp of his jaw before moving round to his nape, almost imperceptibly urging him closer.

'Oh, Grace.' With something like a groan, he pulled her against the length of his body. His arms went round her, holding her tight, and his lips claimed hers in a kiss whose intensity made her senses sing.

Horror in the Darkness

'Wow!' Natasha said. 'You look amazing! Do a twirl, go on.'

Grace laughed, and the scalloped hem of the sleeveless emerald chiffon dress she wore flared out as she spun round. Another of her sister's designs, of course, and it was exquisite. The crystal beadwork round the scoop neckline must have taken hours of hand-sewing.

Following Natasha's advice, she'd put her hair up into a high bun, leaving curling tendrils loose around her face. A velvet headband across her forehead, complete with a sparkling diamanté ornament and ivory-coloured feathers, finished the outfit.

'You're brilliant, Nat,' she said with another laugh. 'We look so nineteen-twenties. Both of us.'

Her sister's dress was rose pink, and made, like Grace's, of soft, floaty chiffon over a cotton voile base the same colour. She, too, wore a headband — a wide band of pink satin with a large oval jewel placed at the centre of her forehead.

From downstairs came the clang of the brass bell that hung outside the château's main entrance, announcing the arrival of more guests to the murder mystery dinner.

Natasha tilted her head, the hint of a frown on her face.

'You look different, Grace. Bubbly. Is there something I should know about?'

Well yes, Grace thought, smiling. She was in love with Kai and he with her, it seemed, and it was the most wonderful thing that had ever happened to her. But she wouldn't share it, not yet, not even with her sister. She wasn't sure she believed it herself yet.

'Maybe.' She felt colour warm her cheeks. 'We'll talk later, OK? Right now, we ought to be making our way downstairs.'

She turned towards the door of her room, but Natasha caught hold of her arm, staying her.

'OK,' she said, and Grace was touched

by the concern she could see in her eyes. 'You can tell me everything later. But take care. Please. Promise?'

Grace didn't hesitate.

'Promise.'

The two of them moved out into the corridor, and Grace locked her bedroom door behind her.

'Have you locked yours?'

Natasha nodded. Angela had asked them to do so. The evening's guests would have a more or less free run of the château, so it made sense to take the precaution of locking their doors. On the first floor, she'd explained, one of Pierre's grandsons would be making sure none of the guests strayed into the family's rooms or Barbs and Johnno's suite.

'Angela's got it all planned out, hasn't she?' Grace said as they headed along the corridor and down the stairs. She could hear music coming up the stair-well from the ground floor, and the buzz of excited chatter. The brass bell rang again as more new arrivals announced their presence.

'Oh, yes,' Natasha replied. 'She's nobody's fool.'

Rounding the bend in the stairs, Grace caught sight of Kai at the very moment he saw her. He smiled up at her — and her heart swooped into a faster beat.

He stood on the first-floor landing. He'd been waiting for her, she thought, filled with happiness at the idea. Cameron was at his side, but her eyes were for Kai alone.

He wore a black dinner jacket with black satin lapels, black trousers turned up at the ankles, a white shirt and waistcoat, and a black bow-tie. His thick hair had been slicked back, giving extra emphasis to the strong lines of his face.

Grace was smiling broadly as she ran the rest of the way down the stairs, coming to a halt so close she was almost touching him.

'You've certainly dressed the part.' It wasn't the run downstairs that made her so breathless. 'You look wonderful.'

He caught her hands in both his.

'So do you.' His eyes didn't leave her face. 'I want to kiss you,' he said softly, for her ears alone, stepping backwards, taking her with him.

'Kai, what . . .' she protested, stumbling, laughing.

But his arms were around her, his mouth on hers, and she gave herself over to the beauty of his kiss.

As if from a great distance came the sound of the double doors opening and closing, Angela's excited greetings, Vespasien's more measured tones.

It was real, she thought, breathing in the smoky notes of Kai's cologne. This amazing feeling was real. She'd imagined herself in love before, but it had never been like this. Natasha was right. She was bubbly. Bubbling over with happiness, and it was the most marvellous feeling ever.

As of one accord, they drew apart. It was time, Grace knew. The noise level from down below was much diminished now. Most of the guests had no doubt moved along to the grand salon.

Kai cupped her face in his hands, kissing the tip of her nose before stepping back.

'I've got to put on my public persona. I'm going to keep my distance, stay away from you. I don't want anyone guessing about us, taking a photo on their phone, selling it to the papers. It's too soon.' Another kiss on her nose. 'Can you understand that?'

With an effort, Grace brought a smile to her face.

'Yes, Kai, I understand.'

She looked around her. They were in a narrow bay about a metre deep, set back from the corridor. A bust of a Roman emperor on a plinth took up about half the space. A curtain, partly shielding them from view, gave a glimpse of the stairs.

A gangling teenager, almost certainly Pierre's grandson, was leaping up them two at a time, followed by Loki, long feather-like tail wagging furiously.

Grace frowned.

'What's Loki doing here? Is Vespasien

all right?' Master and dog were never normally away from each other.

Kai asked the newcomer, receiving a reply in rapid French. He turned to Grace.

'Vespasien's fine. One of the guests doesn't like dogs, that's all. So Loki's going to help keep an eye on the family's rooms.' He caught her hand in his and smiled. 'Shall we join the party?'

She smiled back.

'Yes.'

But he didn't keep her hand in his for long. He didn't want her to be seen with him, with all the attendant publicity and speculation that would provoke, she knew that and understood it. When his hand slid from hers, though, and he moved ahead of her, several stairs below her, she felt bereft, as if a small part of his warmth had left her.

Expelling her breath on a long sigh, she squared her shoulders and continued on down. The hall was empty now. She saw Kai's back as he disappeared past the Christmas tree and through a door, second to last into the grand salon.

Nineteen-twenties jazz was playing. People of all ages were chatting, laughing, joking, waving the glass of kir they held to emphasise their point.

As she threaded her way through the crowd, Grace heard both English and French voices, though she suspected the French guests all spoke good English.

She saw long ropes of pearls, mouths lipsticked into a cupid's bow, cigarette holders brandished airily. Some of the men wore fedoras, brims pulled low. One had a deerstalker. All wore formal suits and starched white shirts. It was clear that everyone had caught the spirit of the event, and Grace felt a thrill of excitement for Angela. Her murder mystery evening was going to be a huge success.

Angela's orange hair had been sculpted into tight waves lying close against the scalp.

'Marcel waves, darling,' she explained. 'All the rage in the twenties. I'm getting into character.'

'You've certainly done that,' Grace

said with a happy smile. 'You look wonderful.'

Kai's mother was resplendent in gold. The fabric of her sleeveless, low-necked gown had a metallic sheen to it and fell in soft flattering folds to her ankles. A gold headband in the form of a snake crossed her forehead while thick snake bangles, also in gold, circled her upper arms.

'It's the Egyptian look,' she said. 'Very fashionable at the time. They'd just discovered Tutankhamun's tomb.'

'Is the dress another of my sister's creations?'

'Of course. Isn't she a marvel? The whole outfit, jewellery as well, cost a fortune though,' she added, voice sinking to a whisper. 'Don't tell Vespi.'

Vespasien stood with his back to the fireplace, a long-stemmed glass in one hand. Like his stepson, he wore black dinner jacket and trousers, white shirt and waistcoat, but with the addition of shiny black patent leather shoes — and a monocle. Grace gave a little laugh of delight.

'Angela insisted,' he said in a tone that was half grumble, half laughter, and Grace was reminded how Kai had said he'd do anything for his wife.

'Looks like an English lord, doesn't he?'

Johnno, joining the two of them, positioned himself just a shade too close to her. She stepped back a pace. Wearing a black fedora and a wide-lapelled suit, brown with white chalk stripes, he looked — very appropriately, Grace couldn't help thinking — the epitome of a 1920s gangster.

'See you're serving the 2005 vintage tonight,' Johnno said to Vespasien, raising the glass he was holding, a third full of red wine. 'Opened a bottle. Tried some of it. Hope you don't mind. Good stuff.' He swallowed a mouthful. 'Not as spectacular as you'd led me to believe, but . . .'

With that, the two men fell into a discussion of vintages, and Grace moved away. Kai, she saw, had put his arm across the shoulder of one of the women he was talking to. But it didn't mean a thing, she told herself, not a thing.

She found Natasha with Cameron and several others at the far end of the grand salon. Earlier in the day, a space had been cleared, and the carpet rolled up and taken away. There'd be dancing here later on in the evening, Grace knew.

Amid much laughter Cameron was teaching Natasha how to do the Charleston. He was a good dancer, Grace saw, and wasn't overly surprised. From the clothes he wore to the paintings and sketches he produced, he was careful and precise at all times.

He'd pencilled in a thin, dark brown moustache above his upper lip.

'Hey, I'm Rudolph Valentino,' he said with a laugh. 'The nineteen-twenties' sexiest heart-throb.'

And all of a sudden Kai was there at her side, the soft wool of his jacket brushing against the bare skin of her arm. He handed her a glass of kir, his fingers touching hers a moment longer than was necessary, and her breath caught in her throat.

'Enjoy,' he said, warm eyes smiling, and then he was gone, pounced on by a woman with kohl-smudged eyes and a beauty spot at the corner of her mouth.

Grace sipped her kir and moved around the room, chatting, joining in. It occurred to her that she was smiling at everyone and everything. But of course she was. She was in love. Kai's touch was fresh in her mind, his scent was on her clothes and on her skin. It was as if he was with her wherever she went.

A gong sounded, the music was turned down low, and an expectant hush fell. All eyes turned toward Angela who now stood by the fireplace next to her husband.

'How lovely to see you all. But I'm not sure you realise what you've let yourselves in for,' she said, good humour in her voice. 'You're going to have a busy evening, darlings. So let's go into the dining-room and when you're all sitting comfortably . . .' a murmur of laughter from some of the older guests '. . . we will begin.'

'She's so good at this sort of thing,' Barbs said into Grace's ear as they moved with everyone else from the grand salon to the dining room. 'Always has been.'

Pierre had extended the table that afternoon and spread a snow-white damask cloth over it. Settings were laid for 11 people either side with one each end, for Vespasien and Angela.

The starter, a selection of seafood on a bed of edible seaweed together with the necessary tools, had already been set out, and by each plate a small envelope.

'Don't open it yet, darlings. Let me explain first.'

Grace found her place and sat down. Kai was diagonally opposite her, she was immensely pleased to see, Cameron was next to her and Natasha a few places further down.

'You've all found the envelope with your name on it,' Angela said when everyone was seated. 'Inside, there's a riddle, a different one for each of you. Your task

162

is to solve it — either before, during or after your starter. It will lead you to a second envelope containing important information about the character you are to play tonight, plus . . .' her voice took on a dramatic note '. . . secret knowledge you have about one or several other people in this room.'

There was a buzz of excited chat. With a smiling glance across the table to Kai, Grace picked up her envelope, opened it and drew out a slip of paper. It read:

'Up and up
And round and round
You do that
And I'll be found'

'Too easy,' Grace said, showing the paper to Cameron at her side. 'It's got to be the tower. The top of the tower.' Warmth crept up over her cheeks as she recalled going there with Kai, the beauty of the view from the top — and the sweet intensity of his kiss.

She looked around at the other guests. Some had clearly decided to have their starter first, attacking oysters and prawns with relish, while others were getting to their feet. Johnno was pouring himself a glass of wine.

She scraped back her chair and stood up. Kai was doing the same. But when she reached the door and glanced back she saw that Barbs had caught his attention and he'd stopped to speak to her.

She hesitated. Should she wait? Together, they could find her second envelope, then his. The thought of stolen moments alone in the tower with Kai was more than tempting. But he was still talking to Barbs, and the decision was made. She wouldn't wait.

They'd accessed the tower via a low door on the second floor, she remembered. The stone steps had gone down as well as up, so logically there had to be an entrance to it on the ground floor, or if not then the first floor, she decided. Taking an instant to orientate herself, she headed along the wide gallery on her left.

And there it was, hidden behind a floor-length velvet curtain, a low door as dark with age as the one on the second floor.

Grace pushed down on the latch and pulled the door open. Recoiling as the cold air and the musty, earthy smell of centuries old stone hit her, she had a moment's misgiving. Perhaps she should have waited for Kai.

Reaching inside, she found the light switch, turned it on, and saw grey-white steps winding upwards. As with the second floor, a thick rope was attached at intervals to the curving outside wall. Closing the door behind her and taking a steadying breath, she grasped the rope in her left hand, placed the palm of her right hand against the central pillar, and started up.

She must have climbed a dozen steps when the light went out. She stilled, instantly, frozen by shock, by sudden fear. Her heart jolted in a single sickening thump.

It was pitch black. There were no windows, no arrow slits that starlight could filter through. She was effectively blind.

The rough rope in one hand, the cold stone against the palm of the other, the solid step beneath her feet — they were her only points of reference.

Continue on up? Or go back down? She had to be nearer the first floor than the ground, she reasoned. There'd be a door, wouldn't there? Or a light switch.

Up.

Her heart was pounding an uneasy rhythm. She lifted one foot on to the step above, slid her hand along the rope, the other up the central pillar, then brought the second foot up on to the same step.

Her tension eased a fraction. So far, so good. Do it again. And again. Step by slow step she made her way up the tower. She had to be almost at the first floor by now. And that was when it happened, in a tangled confusion of thoughts and events.

The sound of breathing. Hers? No. Someone else. Kai! It had to be, and her pulses leaped. An arm reaching out. The soft wool of his jacket against her arm. Kai had come for her. He'd get her out of here. A faint whiff of his cologne — from her skin? Or from his?

No. How could it be? He was grabbing her. Pushing her. She heard a grunt of effort. And with a cry she was going down. The air whooshed from her lungs as her body came down hard, and she slithered, crashing from side to side like a dodgem car gone mad, elbows cracking against the stone steps and walls, spine jarring against the sharp edge of each and every step.

Kai had pushed her, she thought as she came to a juddering halt, and her disbelief was total. The man she loved had pushed her.

Sinister Discovery

Grace groaned. She knew she had to stay still. She could hear footsteps running, coming her way. Then Kai appeared in the open doorway — and she flinched. She couldn't help it. It was an instinctive reaction.

He frowned. Reaching inside, he flicked the switch. The light came on. One look at his face when he saw her lying there and she knew she'd been wrong to doubt him.

'Grace, sweetheart.' Pulling off his jacket, he knelt down beside her, spreading it over her, tucking it in round her shoulders. 'Tell me you're OK.' There was desperation in his voice. His face had lost all colour.

His brother appeared at his side.

'Cam, call one-five. Get an ambulance here.'

'No,' Grace murmured. 'I'm fine.' It was an effort to speak. 'No bones broken.'

'You can't know that, sweetheart.' Kai's tone was soothing as he brushed strands of hair back from her face. 'Let's get you checked over at the hospital.'

'Don't tell Angela. This dinner's important to her. I don't want to spoil it for her.'

He frowned.

'All right. If that's what you want.'

'I didn't fall, Kai. I was pushed.' She saw his expression harden and he started to get to his feet. She touched her hand to his sleeve. 'There's something else.'

'What?'

She swallowed.

'I thought it was you who'd pushed me.' She paused, plunged on, mouth dry. 'Swear to me it wasn't.'

His head jerked back as if she'd landed a punch to the jaw.

'You really need to ask?' His voice was a growl.

She could see the hurt in his eyes. She wished she hadn't spoken. Shock, perhaps, had put the words into her mouth.

'I'm sorry.'

169

'Why on earth would you think I was the one who pushed you?'

'I . . .' She was close to tears. 'It was so dark. Pitch black. Your jacket, the sleeve of your jacket, I felt it.' She hesitated, shaken still. 'And I could smell your cologne.'

He sat back on his heels, shaking his head.

'You could have been killed.'

'I was lucky. I fell feet first. On my back.' She shivered, remembering.

'Head first and you might not be here to tell the tale.' His tone was grim. Anger had replaced the hurt. 'Someone did this to you, someone wanted to kill you, and we need to find out who.'

Abruptly, he stood up, taking the phone out of his pocket. He tapped a two-figure number into his phone and was soon speaking in fluent French to the person at the other end of the line. At last he snapped the phone shut and took her hands in his.

'The gendarmes will take a statement from you at the hospital. Two of them.

They both speak English. Security there is excellent, they say. You'll be perfectly safe.'

Grace absorbed the words, saw the concern in Kai's eyes, and a shudder coursed through her body. For, of course, she was still in danger — just so long as her assailant remained uncaught.

★ ★ ★

'How are you feeling this morning?'

'Nat!' Grace winced as she pushed herself into a sitting position, smiling with pleasure as her sister came into the hospital room carrying a bag and a bunch of flowers.

Natasha put the bag down on the bed.

'Clothes. Skinny jeans, brown boots, underwear, and the sweater with the penguin on it — because it's Christmas Eve,' she added with a laugh. 'And these are from guess-who,' she said, handing the flowers to her sister. The cellophane they were wrapped in rustled and crackled. 'Lucky you.'

Roses, a beautiful deep pinky-orange colour. Grace held them to her nose, inhaling the sweet scent and, inexplicably, she felt tears well in her eyes as her thoughts went back to the previous evening.

He'd knelt beside her on the cold floor at the foot of the tower, stroking her hands, murmuring soft words. Natasha had arrived at the same time as the ambulance. Maybe he'd texted her or sent Cameron to fetch her, Grace didn't know.

'Stay with her until the gendarmes have been and gone,' he'd said to Natasha, getting to his feet. 'Keep her safe for me,' he had added.

'Why? Aren't you coming with me?' Grace had asked.

He shook his head. The look he turned on her and his voice when he spoke were steely with determination.

'I've got things to do here.'

At the hospital Grace had been x-rayed and scanned, and had been given the all-clear. The doctor who'd examined her had asked some very searching questions, no doubt worried she was in an abusive relationship.

Grace suspected she would have called the gendarmes if they hadn't in fact turned up 15 minutes later. She'd told them everything she could remember, and Kai had been right, they spoke very good English.

'You didn't answer my question.' Her sister's voice broke into her thoughts, bringing her back to the present. 'How are you feeling?'

'Battered and bruised, a bit shaken still, but otherwise OK. They wanted to keep me in overnight just to double-check, but I'm fine. Really I am.'

'Your dress isn't. I took it back with me last night. I'm not sure I'm going to be able to repair it. You know,' she continued, 'I don't think we should wait till the twenty-sixth. I think we should go back to the UK today.'

'No.' Grace was shaking her head.

'We can leave here then collect our stuff from the château. You stay in the

173

car while I sort it with everyone, then we head off up to . . .'

'No. No, Natasha.' She stopped for an instant, thinking, putting some of the pieces of the jigsaw together in her mind. 'I originally thought getting that electric shock was an accident. But now I'm not so sure. Being pushed down the stairs of the tower was definitely not an accident. It was a deliberate act.'

'All the more reason to leave.'

'No,' Grace repeated with a determined shake of her head. 'I need to find out why. Why me? Why have I been targeted? I must go back to the château.'

She couldn't prevent the shiver that chilled her skin despite the warmth of the hospital room. She was scared, and wasn't afraid to admit it to herself. It was the only way, though. She had to do it.

'Listen, Nat,' she went on. 'I don't want you to stay with me. The roads are clear. Go on up to the port, get the ferry home.'

'No, Grace.' Natasha's turn to shake her head. 'You're my little sister. I'm not leaving you here alone.'

Grace was moved beyond words. She reached for her sister just as Natasha's arms came round her, wrapping her in a tight hug, and the tears that had been threatening all night spilled at last down her cheeks.

★ ★ ★

Kai didn't speak until he'd closed the door to the barn that housed the family's cars behind the two of them. Natasha had stayed with Angela and Vespasien, bringing them up to date.

'Nothing but negatives so far,' he said as they set off across the snow, heading for the forest's edge. They walked side by side, not touching, and Grace was uneasy, missing the way he'd always thrown his arm across her shoulders, drawing her to him.

He was the other reason she'd had to come back to the château, of course. She wanted her time with him to last for as long as possible. She couldn't bear to cut it short.

He could have his pick of any woman in the world. He'd soon tire of ordinary, unremarkable her. But until then she had to make the most of every moment she had with him. While it lasted.

Perhaps the relationship — brief as it was — was waning already, she thought, and her heart was heavy at the prospect.

Heavy grey-white clouds hung low in the sky, threatening snow. A cold little breeze played over the exposed skin of her face. The cawing of rooks as they flew from one treetop to the next pierced the silence of the land around them.

'I found the piece of paper with the riddle you were given,' he said. 'It was about halfway up the tower, between the ground and first floors.'

'I must have dropped it,' she murmured, 'when he made a grab at me.'

'Grace, my sweet.' She heard the pain in his voice, then his arms went round her, pulling her against him, and he was rocking her from side to side. The bruises down her back protested but she didn't mind. She didn't mind at all. He pressed kisses to her face, her hair, and all at once her spirits were soaring. She barely registered his words.

'What you must have gone through — I blame myself. I should have been there.'

'Kai, no. It was my fault. I should have waited for you.'

Keeping her within the circle of his arms, he lifted his head from hers, and brushed the tears from her cheeks with the pad of his thumb.

'Don't cry, sweetheart. You're safe now.'

They walked on as snowflakes began to fall. Both his arms were round her, clasping her to his side. She leaned her head against his shoulder. The aches in her body were forgotten, and she found she was smiling — from the sheer pleasure of being held by the man she loved.

'The door that leads to the first floor,' he said a while later, 'is set back from the staircase. That's where he or she must have been hiding. They turned the lights off, then lay in wait.'

'He. It was a man. I heard him grunt.'

'Did you tell the police that?'

She thought back.

'Yes.'

'Good.' He paused, clearly gathering his thoughts then spoke again. 'I went on up to the top of the tower, looked all over but there wasn't a second envelope anywhere. The riddle sent you on a wild goose chase, its sole aim to get you into the tower.'

Grace shuddered as the memory of that wild, slithering fall came flashing back into her mind, and Kai's hands closed even more tightly round her upper arm.

'I had a word with Vespasien and my mother. A quiet word because the murder mystery dinner was still going on and you were right, it meant a lot to my mother. It was going very well. I didn't want to ruin it for her.'

'You did the right thing, Kai.' The snow was falling more thickly now, settling on their heads and shoulders.

'I told them what had happened, and they were shocked. Horrified. My mother went white. They confirmed what I already knew — they weren't the ones who'd written the 'up and up' riddle.'

'So someone substituted their own riddle for the one Angela and Vespasien had put in the envelope?'

He nodded.

'They'd prepared a different one for you — one that wouldn't have taken you to the tower at all, but to the second-floor landing. I went up there and found the second envelope where they'd said it would be, taped to the back of the painting of Napoleon winning the battle of Austerlitz.'

'I know the one you mean. You know,' she went on, speaking slowly, thinking as she spoke, 'it all comes back to paintings, doesn't it? Or rather, a painting. The badly restored Sisley.' She twisted in his arms so that she could see his face. 'I think we need to have another look at the Sisley.'

He took her hand in his as they retraced their steps across the snow, through the barn and covered walkway and into the kitchen. There, they pulled off hats, coats and gloves, leaving them draped over chairs.

Urgency gave Grace speed. Kai, too — no doubt for the same reason. Were they at last about to find the explanation for — what? The accidents that had befallen her? The attempts on her life? It was impossible to take it in. Grace's mind shied away.

The two of them met no-one on their way to the corridor that led to the dining-room.

The first time Grace had noticed the painting, she'd given voice to little more than fleeting impressions. When Cameron returned it to its position on the wall, almost completely hidden by a vase of holly, she'd barely glanced at it on her way in to or out of dinner.

But now, as she and Kai came to a halt in front of it, she took several long, steadying breaths, forcing herself to slow down, to give herself the time to examine the painting properly.

She wondered at the holly, all glossy, spiky leaves and fat red berries, that had replaced the flowers. Could it be there to discourage people from peering too closely at the painting, she couldn't help thinking as she lifted the vase. Kai took it from her and set it down on the ground further along.

The light was poor here, and Grace unhooked the Sisley, turning it over to see a couple of old auction labels on the back. Carrying it over to the window, she angled the painting as she studied it. Though muted by the falling snow, the even, northern light was an improvement.

The painting showed a country lane running diagonally across the canvas, bordered on both sides by leafy chestnut trees. A woman leaning back against the trunk of one of the trees gave human scale to the landscape while two other figures, made tiny by distance, could be seen at the far end of the lane.

Grace saw again the inconsistencies that had caught her eye that first time, the green that was just a shade too bright, and the little curls of white paint on the lane which had struck her as more consistent with Sisley's later style.

But it was something else she saw now, something that drained the colour from her face.

'This isn't a badly restored painting, Kai.' He stood behind her, hands curling round her upper arms.

'That should be good news.' His tone told her he knew it wasn't. Tears filled her eyes. She blinked them back.

'It's a copy,' she said. 'And I know who made it.'

'Tell me.'

Holding the painting so the lower edge of the frame rested against her stomach, she pointed with her free hand.

'The two men there, in the distance. They're holding hands.' She sucked in a breath. She couldn't even begin to work out all the implications. Not yet.

'Sisley would never have painted that,'

she said, shaking her head as a tear slid down her cheek. 'Cameron did.'

Accusations and Denials

'Let me take that.' Without waiting for an answer, Kai took the Sisley from her and tucked it under one arm.

'Kai. Where are we going?' He'd grasped her hand, was drawing her at speed towards the château's main staircase. The bruises on her arms and legs protested furiously.

'To his studio. It's mid-morning. That's where he'll be.' His hand was like a manacle round hers. Every inch of his body spoke of steel determination.

'Kai, please. Maybe it's not what we think.'

'You mean, my brother didn't set out to kill you?'

She could hear the anguish in his words, saw it in his eyes when they reached the stairs and he looked quickly back at her.

'That's quite a leap,' she said. She was breathless and her voice shook. 'From knowing the painting's a copy to . . .' A leap she too had made, she knew, and a sick feeling swirled again in her stomach.

He started up the stairs, taking her with him, and she dragged at his hand, slowing the pace.

'Don't hurt him, Kai. Please.'

Another quick look back at her.

'I mean to find out the truth. Come on.' He tugged at her hand, and she found she had to run, taking the stairs two at a time to keep up.

'I've come to no harm.' Her words came in gasps as they rounded the bend in the stairs and headed up the second flight. 'I'm all right, Kai. Promise me you won't hurt him.'

He didn't answer, and Grace's heart was thumping a fast uneven beat when they arrived outside the door to the studio.

He didn't knock, simply twisted the knob and pushed the door open.

Cameron stood at an easel, his back to them, palette in one hand, brush in the other. He jumped, turning his head to the door, clearly startled.

In one swift movement Kai had put the painting down on the floor, let go Grace's hand and was crossing the room to his brother.

'Hey . . .' Cam got no further.

'Tell me the truth.' Kai had caught hold of the neck of his brother's shirt in one hand, and was forcing him backwards against the dresser. His other hand was bunched in a fist at his side. Grace's pulse raced, shocked by the sudden violence and by his anger, thrumming through the air. 'Tell me you didn't push her down the stairs.'

'Are you crazy? No! Of course I didn't.' His gaze flicked wildly from Kai to Grace and back to Kai. All colour had left his face. The palette and brush had dropped, bouncing, to the floor. 'What's all this about?'

'The Sisley's a copy.'

'OK, yes. I admit it. But that doesn't mean I'm going to go round pushing people down stairs.'

He spoke fast, as though desperate to convince, and darted pleading looks at Grace who'd remained by the door. Relief washed over her. She needed no more convincing.

'Let go of him, Kai. He's telling the truth.' She had no doubt of it.

For long moments Kai didn't move. His stance as he held his brother pinned against the dresser remained as rigid as before. His eyes stayed fixed on Cameron's face, as if searching his features for clues.

Then, at last, Grace saw the tension ease from his shoulders, and the hand that held the neck of Cameron's shirt slid away, letting go.

'Very well,' he said, flexing the fingers of both hands as he stepped back a pace. 'You've said you had nothing to do with it, and I accept what you say.'

There was a touch of theatricality in the way his brother rubbed his throat, brushed down his paint-spattered shirt and bent to pick up his brush and palette. Luckily it had landed paint side up.

'Thanks a million,' he said. Unusually for him, he hadn't shaved that morning and looked rather the worse for wear, Grace thought.

'You had no reason to push me down the tower,' she said, speaking slowly, working it out as she spoke. Whoever had tried to kill her, it wasn't Kai's brother, and the relief of knowing that was like a heady rush of alcohol to her bloodstream.

'This business with the Sisley, it's not a secret you've got to protect at all costs. After all, you put your signature . . .' she sketched quote marks in the air '. . . in plain sight.'

'The two men holding hands. Yes.'

Grace saw the small, complacent smile that curved Cameron's mouth, and more pieces of the jigsaw fell into place.

'You almost want to be found out, don't you? You want the world — and Vespasien especially — to know how clever you are. How talented you are,' she said, using the word that had caused those awkward moments at dinner — how many evenings ago?

Cameron flushed.

'He never looks at his paintings.'

'He doesn't appreciate them. They're investments,' he finished, giving bitter emphasis to the last word, and darting a quick glance at his brother who stood, tall and unyielding, less than a metre from him.

Kai had his hands in his pockets, thumbs hooked through the belt loops of his trousers. He was listening intently, Grace sensed, and watching the play of emotions across his brother's face.

'In fact,' she said, 'I bet you used the wrong green and those short curling brushstrokes deliberately — little anachronistic details that would make a fool of him when they were found out, as of course they surely would be if he ever tried to sell the painting.'

'Is Grace right?' Kai spoke quietly. A deceptive calm, Grace thought. 'Is that why you did it? Copied the Sisley?'

Cameron nodded, chin tilting up in a small show of defiance.

'Have you done any more?'

Grace saw Cameron hesitate before

he spoke, reluctantly.

'I'm working on one at the moment.'

'Show me.'

Another hesitation. Then, twisting round, he crouched down, opened one of the doors of the lower part of the dresser and drew out two rectangular shapes covered in cloth.

Curious, Grace crossed the room to join the two brothers. He'd accidentally left the door ajar, she recalled, that morning she, Kai and Natasha had spent in his studio, had coloured and pushed it closed with his foot. She'd supposed, she remembered thinking, that the canvases covered in cloth had something to do with his lover. Obviously not, she now decided, watching as he removed one of the cloths.

It was another early Sisley, still in its frame, showing a footpath along a river or stream, with trees and a tumbledown cottage in the middle ground.

'He hasn't even noticed it's gone,' Cameron said. Handing the Sisley to Grace, he removed the second cloth.

'Here's my version. It's almost finished.'

Kai put his arm across Grace's shoulders, drawing her to him. She glanced up, saw his gaze flick from one painting to the other, comparing the original and the copy Cameron was holding out.

'I must admit,' Kai said, 'it's good.'

'I've studied his technique.'

'Ah, so now we know,' Grace said, 'why only Sisleys get — quote — restored. Oh!' All at once she stopped. A chill of unease sped down her spine.

Kai pointed to two tiny figures, both men, standing hand in hand by the door of the tumbledown cottage.

'You say Vespasien never looks at his paintings, but you're chancing your arm with this.'

'I don't care any more,' Cameron said.

'You're making the announcement.' It was a statement, not a question.

'Yes. It's my New Year's resolution. I'm moving in with . . . him.'

Grace was only half-listening to what the two brothers were saying, only half-registered the defensiveness that had entered Cameron's voice. A growing dread of what was to come was seeping into her bones, and she twisted away from Kai. His arm fell to his side, leaving a chill across her shoulders where the warmth and weight of it had been.

'In the meantime,' he was saying, 'you're going to put the Sisley originals back where they belong. Today.'

'I can't do that. I can't put chestnut trees back.'

Grace hugged her arms across her chest. If only she'd never drawn attention to the Sisley. Or, having done so, why couldn't she have said moments later with a laugh that she'd been wrong? If only!

She heard Kai swear.

'Why on earth not?' She held her breath.

'Because our dear mama has sold it.'

The words dropped like a rock into still water. Cameron fell silent. Kai stared at him, frowning, shaking his head. And Grace wished she could vanish in a puff of smoke. She'd never wanted to cause such hurt to the man she loved.

'Sold it to a private collector,' Cameron was saying. 'Someone Johnno knows.'

Kai turned pained eyes on Grace, and she knew the implications were sinking in. She'd dismissed the notion that a woman had pushed her down the tower steps. Only Kai had entertained that possibility — and perhaps he'd been right to do so.

She swallowed against the painful ache in her throat.

'I'm sorry, Kai.'

'Hey, no. She'd never do that.'

How Grace hoped he was right. But of course Angela had to be involved. She was the one who'd spoken of the painting being sent away to be restored, had tried to make light of the whole subject.

Grace thought, too, of the old auction labels on the back of the painting she'd examined, and was in no doubt Angela and Cameron had set out deliberately to deceive Vespasien into thinking the copy — the fake — was a genuine Sisley.

She looked at Kai's grim face, and a sick dread swirled uneasily through her. This was not going to end well.

There was contempt in the look he directed at his brother.

'Let's get this straight.' His voice was cold as steel. 'You painted a copy, and it was kept here on the walls of the château. Angela sold the original. Correct?'

Cameron nodded.

'You intend doing the same with this second one?'

Another nod.

'Well, it's not going to happen.' Kai took his phone out of his pocket, flipped it open. 'At least she didn't sell the copy. Small mercies.'

The phone call to his mother was brief and curt.

'She'll be here shortly,' he said, putting the phone back in his pocket. With the heel of his boot, he hooked a chair out from under a table covered in tubes of paint and pots of brushes, turned it round and sat, legs apart, forearms resting on his thighs.

His head was bowed, and Grace couldn't begin to guess what he was going through.

Suspicion had been thrown first at his brother, now at his mother. She put her arms across his shoulders and pressed a kiss to the back of his neck.

'What a mess,' he murmured, giving her arm a brief squeeze before letting his hand drop back down between his knees. There was a finality in the way he spoke, she thought, and the ache in her throat grew more painful still as she realised he didn't want her close.

They waited.

With a heavy heart, Grace moved round the studio. Glancing up at the high window, she saw the sky was white with snowflakes, carried this way and that like a flock of starlings by the gusting wind.

Leaning back against the dresser, Cameron was muttering, not so much to be heard, more to fill the silence, Grace guessed. Perhaps to break the tension that gripped the room.

'This hasn't improved my hang-over . . . supposed to be something special . . . rough old stuff . . .'

'Shut it, Cam.' Kai's voice was a growl.

Grace looked round at Cameron's paintings, the two Sisley copies, his clever Paris places and faces sketches, his current work in progress, a moody abstract.

He was a talented, versatile artist, she thought, and hoped he'd soon find his way — a way that didn't involve deception and petty revenge on a disliked stepfather.

Angela arrived at last, sweeping in through the door with a swish of satin and a flurry of movement. She wasn't beaming her usual smile. Kai's tone over the phone must have warned her.

She looked round, gaze fixing for a fraction of a second on each person in the room before dropping to the three paintings — Cameron's two copies and the Sisley original — now on the floor propped against the dresser. She turned to Kai.

'I had to do it, darling. Vespi's cut my

monthly allowance. Drastically. I . . .'

'It's the last time you sell any of his paintings,' Kai cut in, sitting back in his chair. He spoke quickly, like a man wanting to get the nuts and bolts business over with as soon as possible. 'Or any of the treasures round here. That's a given. Understood? If you want money, ask me.'

'But I . . .'

'I need to know how far you were prepared to go to protect your secret.'

'I . . . what?' Angela frowned, looking with worried eyes from one brother to the other. 'What do you mean? What are you getting at?'

'Did you push Grace down the stairs in the tower?'

There was an instant's disbelieving hush before Angela spoke.

'No!' Angela stepped back, shaking her head, over and over. 'No, of course not!' Her gaze darted from Kai to Grace and back to Kai. 'No, I could never do that! Kai.' There was desperation in her voice. 'Kai, say you believe me.'

He briefly closed his eyes, tilting his head back, and his relief was almost tangible.

'Of course I believe you,' he said gruffly, as he got to his feet and crossed to his mother, wrapping her in a hug, burying his face in her hair.

Tears filled Grace's eyes. The ache in her throat made it almost impossible to swallow. With a quick glance at Cameron, she turned to the door. There was no place for her here.

The Awful Truth Dawns

Grace drew in a shuddering breath before continuing her story. Her voice was thick. Tears weren't far from the surface.

'Kai asked Angela how far she'd go to protect her secret, and it was obvious she didn't have the faintest idea what he was going on about.'

'But that's good, Grace. Isn't it?' There was concern in Natasha's voice, and she reached across, taking her sister's hands in hers and giving them a strength-imparting squeeze.

They were sitting side by side in armchairs — small upholstered chairs with padded arms — by the window of Grace's bedroom, looking out over the château's park. Snow, smooth and untouched, covered everything, reminding Grace of the day they'd arrived. How much had happened since!

She looked now at Natasha.

'Of course it's good. I could see she

was sincere, and I was so, so happy she wasn't the one that had pushed me.' A single tear spilled and she brushed it away. 'She sold the Sisley to a private collector Johnno helped her find. For less than market value, I imagine. If she'd tried to sell at auction, there'd have been publicity, and Vespasien might have heard about it.'

She paused, sniffed, cuffed away another tear.

'Then Kai wrapped his arms round her, and Cameron was about to hug the two of them, and it was so moving to see, I was close to tears. And that's when I had to leave.' She looked again at Natasha, glad of the warmth of her sister's hands round hers.

'I wasn't part of it, Nat. And I don't think I'll ever be a part of his life. I don't belong here. I keep telling myself to make the most of the time I have with him, but it's no use. I want to mean more to him than just a quick fling. And of course I never will.'

'You can't know that,' Natasha protested.

'I've brought nothing but disruption and upset to his life . . .'

'That's not your fault. He's hardly likely to blame you, is he?'

Grace shook her head.

'I don't know. I just don't know.'

She fell silent, conscious of the thoughts and doubts and emotions crowding her mind, and she couldn't rid herself of the notion that the happiest chapter of her life was drawing to an unwanted close.

Outside, the snow had almost stopped. Snowflakes zigzagged lazily down to the ground. Grace looked over to her right where the dark trees of the forest stood motionless, spattered by lines of white along their branches.

She and Kai had walked the pathways there, hand in hand, or wrapped in each other's arms. They'd talked and laughed, breathing in the crisp country air, and it had been a wonderful, magical time.

She looked in the other direction, at

the vineyard-covered hills on her left. They had yet to explore those gentle slopes. But with a small sound of annoyance, she caught herself up. That would never happen. She and Kai would never walk there together.

'I want us to go home, Nat,' she now said. 'As soon as we can.'

'I'm fine with that — we still don't know who tried to kill you. We're best out of here. It won't be today, though.'

Grace bit her lip.

'As soon as the roads are cleared.' The fact that her assailant remained at large seemed of little consequence. What did matter was that she was trapped, here at the château — with her memories, and with the man to whom she'd brought nothing but unhappiness.

'Grace . . .' Natasha's voice had taken on an added seriousness. 'I think you're wrong about Kai. Will you promise me one thing?'

'What?'

'That you'll hear what he has to say before we leave?'

True to her word, Grace sought Kai out after lunch, a ham and cheese sandwich each that Natasha popped down to the kitchen to make, and that they ate in her sister's room. Conscious that her unhappiness was written in every feature of her face, Grace hadn't wanted to risk meeting anyone, and least of all Kai.

After lunch, a shower and a change of clothes, though, she felt stronger, more able to face him. Together with Natasha, she followed the sounds of his guitar as they made their way downstairs.

The music came in short bursts. He'd play the same few bars several times, then with a subtle variation. He was clearly working on a new song, one whose haunting, evocative notes threatened to bring fresh tears to her eyes.

The two sisters stopped outside the petit salon.

'I'll be in the kitchen,' Natasha whispered just as the air was filled with the discordant clash of all twelve strings being strummed at once.

Grace's heart was beating fast as, with a single knock, she pushed the door open.

He was alone, sitting — as she'd seen so often — with the ankle of one leg resting on the knee of the other, his guitar across his lap. He looked up as she came in, putting his guitar aside and getting to his feet in one fluid movement.

Grace faltered, confused, not understanding. He'd seen who'd come in and his face had lit up, she was certain. She glanced down at his guitar, giving herself a mental shake, and when she looked at him again, she knew she'd been mistaken. He wore the polite smile of an acquaintance. No more.

'Natasha and I will be leaving as soon as the roads are clear. Tomorrow, I hope.'

Kai's eyebrow went up.

'Do the ferries run on Christmas Day?'

'I don't know. Easy enough to go online and find out,' Grace said, horribly aware that there was an awkwardness between them that hadn't been there before.

They stood facing each other, less than a metre apart, and the smoky notes of his cologne mingled with the scents of the oak logs burning in the fireplace.

'It's for the best,' he said. 'We're no closer to knowing who it was that pushed you down the stairs.'

'At least we know it had nothing to do with the Sisley.'

'True.' He was then silent, and Grace knew he, too, was thinking back to the awful scenes that had taken place in his brother's studio.

A log shifted in the grate.

'So it must have been something else I saw. Something I heard, maybe.' After all the hours they'd shared, how could she sound so stilted with him?

Her heart was aching. She longed to reach out, to take his hand in hers, or run her fingertips along the line of his jaw and up into his hair, to try to recapture that sense of closeness she'd felt so often with him.

With a sound low in his throat, he part-turned away, pushing fingers like claws through his hair.

'I don't want to go through anything like that ever again.' He turned back, his gaze holding hers. 'I wish . . .' His hand came up, and Grace's pulse leaped. Had he read her mind? Did he, like her, long to take her hand in his? Trail his fingers over her face and into her hair?

'I wish,' he said, 'that we could put the clock back to the start of the morning, rerun this whole business with my brother and mother. Better still, if none of it had ever happened.'

His hand dropped back to his side, and Grace felt the loss as acutely as if he'd been holding her tight in his arms, then let her go.

'But it did happen, Kai,' she said quietly. 'We can't undo it.'

He said nothing. His eyes still held hers. His smile was bleak. From outside came a flurry of footsteps, and the door to the petit salon was flung open. Cameron.

'Hey, sorry,' he said, glancing from his brother to Grace. 'I'm not interrupting anything, am I?'

'No,' Grace said, and the weight of sorrow — the sorrow of what might have been — made every word an effort. 'Nothing at all.'

* * *

'We're stuck here,' Natasha said, 'and we'll just have to make the best of it. All of us,' she went on. 'If I know Angela, she'll be playing it as if nothing's happened. She'll be bright and gushing, and every other word will be 'darling'.'

Grace smiled at the mental picture her sister was painting, and was amazed that, somehow, she too could act as if nothing had happened.

The two of them were in Natasha's room, getting ready for the Réveillon, the big Christmas celebration meal for family and friends that would go on till midnight and beyond.

'After all,' Natasha continued, 'she won't want Vespasien to know anything's up. Cameron will be — Cameron,' she

207

said with a laugh, 'and Kai ...' The laughter left her voice. 'Well, he'll be back to being Mr Moody, I imagine.'

Kai. Throughout the afternoon, the sound of his guitar had drifted up the central staircase, filling the château with the haunting notes of the melody he'd been working on earlier. From time to time she thought she heard his deep growl of a voice as he sang. And, too, the discordant clash of all twelve strings played at once that spoke of anger vented.

Kai. How was she going to survive — what? Four hours? Five? — in the same room as him when her heart was breaking? When all she longed for was to be in his arms again.

At eight, dressed in the deep pinky-red two-piece she'd worn the first evening at the château, she went downstairs and along to the petit salon with Natasha. To her dismay, her eyes went directly to Kai, tall and lean, and devastatingly attractive in his black dinner jacket and trousers, white shirt and waistcoat, and black bow-tie.

Their eyes met across the room, her breath caught in her throat, and it was an effort to look away.

Natasha had been right about Angela. Splendidly flamboyant in sapphire blue silk that rustled and fluttered with every movement, she was the perfect hostess, ensuring that everyone mingled and no-one felt left out.

So Grace made small talk, though she was certain she would never be able to recall a word she'd said or heard, not even five minutes later. She even welcomed it when Johnno corralled her into a corner.

'Itching to propose a toast,' he said, raising his glass of kir. 'Vesp doesn't want any fuss made, though.' He nodded towards his host who stood with his back to the fireplace, Loki asleep at his feet, talking to Barbs.

'Ah.' She could hear Kai's deep tones from the other side of the room. He had his back to her, was talking to his brother.

'Got the e-mail this afternoon. Three hundred cases of the 2005 red. Vesp's

best ever vintage. Business acquaintance of mine. Pleased as Punch. Got it
for what the French call an interesting
price.' Chuckling, he leaned closer, and
placed his hand high on the wall beside
her. To bar her escape? Grace wondered.
She could smell the cigarette smoke on
his clothes.

Sensing movement, she looked past
him — and couldn't help smiling. She
didn't need it but Kai, her knight in
shining armour, had come to the rescue.

'Hmm.' Johnno was looking behind
him. 'Time for another ciggie, maybe.'

Kai followed with his eyes as Johnno
threaded his way through the salon.
Grace thought he was about to say something to her. But, with a brief, neutral
smile, he turned and walked away.

'Was Johnno propositioning you?' her
sister asked moments later as they all
left the petit salon, heading for the dining-room.

Grace shook her head.

'Boasting about some deal he's helped
make.'

Natasha laughed.

'Another dodgy deal?'

The dining table glittered and glowed. Slender white candles in gold candelabra threw a softly-flickering light over fine gold-rimmed china and long-stemmed glasses. The warm, spicy scents of pine, cloves and orange filled the air. Christmas music played low in the background.

Grace took her place at the table. Kai sat down opposite her, the last thing she wanted. The play of candlelight over his features took her breath away. Her throat was aching, and she lowered her head.

She ate mechanically, barely registering the food or the conversations going on around her or the clack of knives and forks on china, and forced herself not to think about Kai.

Her mind went back to her sister's throwaway remark. Yes, Johnno had helped Angela sell a painting that wasn't hers to sell, thus proving he wasn't above a little dishonesty. And he'd said Vespasien didn't want a fuss made over his wine sale. So, was there something dodgy about this deal, too?

Three hundred cases of the 2005 red. Vespasien's best ever vintage, Johnno had said. Were there six bottles or 12 in a case? Either way, it meant an awful lot of wine, and all sold at a price cheaper than the going rate for an exceptional vintage.

She watched Kai stand up and leave the room, heading upstairs, at Angela's request, to fetch a stole for his mother. The longing for what might have been was constantly on her mind.

Cameron, sitting on Grace's right, nudged her and handed her a bottle of wine, indicating with a nod that she should pass it on down to Johnno. Grace looked at the label as she did so, and an image came to her.

The afternoon of their arrival at the château, when Vespasien had shown them round the wine cellars, she'd happened to see a pile of labels on the desk, and he'd snapped at her and taken them from her. She could picture them clearly, even now, several days later — the familiar pen-and-ink drawing of the château's façade, the words Château Beauvallon, and the year. 2005.

She frowned, unease prickling across the back of her neck. Something was wrong there. A 2005 vintage would have been bottled and labelled in 2006, wouldn't it? Why would anyone be labelling a 2005 vintage now, 12 years later?

And all at once she understood. A shiver ran down her spine despite the warmth of the room. She looked along the table, at the man who sat at its head, the man who was cheating his customers.

Vespasien Beauvallon de Mottefort. The man who had tried to kill her.

An Impossible Romance

His eyes met hers in an instant that lasted an age. She saw the jolt of recognition in them. He'd seen that eureka moment, knew she'd found him out, and there was anger in the hardening of his expression.

She looked away, down at her plate. What was she to do? What should she do for the best? Accuse him there and then? In front of his family and guests?

No. She couldn't do it. Couldn't bring yet more upset, disruption and, yes, ugliness to Kai's family. Ignore it? Of course not.

That left only one option.

She drew in a long breath, gathering her courage. Her eyes never left his as she dropped her serviette on to her plate, pushed back her chair and got to her feet.

She hesitated for the barest fraction of a second. Should she wait for Kai to come back? Or gesture to Natasha to come with her? No. This was something she had to deal with alone.

Her heartbeat was loud in her ears as she made for the door and the corridor outside, knowing Vespasien would follow. She heard the dining-room door close behind him and spun round to face him.

'I should have guessed way before now, shouldn't I?' She spoke with quiet vehemence, angry as much with herself as with him. 'When I first saw the labels over there in the wine cellars. You overreacted and snatched them from me. That should have told me there was something wrong.'

'My mistake,' Vespasien murmured, looking her full in the face, not at all contrite. From the other side of the dining-room door came the muted sounds of people talking, the odd burst of laughter, and Loki's plaintive high-pitched whine.

She'd been thinking of Kai, Grace recalled, moving further down the wide corridor, in the opposite direction from the central hall.

'So you've been relabelling other bottles. Or you've bought wine in from somewhere else and put your own labels on. Which is it?'

They had come to a halt several metres from the dining-room door and stood facing each other. Vespasien didn't answer straight away. Pulling at his shirt cuffs, he inspected the sleeves of his jacket.

'Relabelling the 2013, mademoiselle' he admitted at last. 'It wasn't a good year.'

'Passing inferior wine off as an exceptional vintage. Selling cheaper stuff at an inflated price.'

'And about to make a tidy profit. Thanks to Johnno, I have a buyer all lined up.'

There was an arrogance, a total lack of remorse about him that threatened to break Grace's self-control. Her hands clenched at her sides.

'And for that you were prepared to kill me.'

He flinched, and ugly colour stained

his cheeks. Grace could hear Loki scrabble at the dining-room door, desperate to join his master.

'No. Not kill you,' Vespasien said. 'Just drive you away.' Another pause. 'It was an impulse. A moment of madness that I've regretted ever since.'

Grace's eyebrows shot up.

'An impulse that took some planning, surely.'

'No.' Looking down, he pushed the fingertips of one hand hard across his forehead. All at once his arrogance was gone, and Grace felt the tension ease from her shoulders.

'Angela wanted to change into her outfit,' he said. 'She asked me to print out the riddles and put them in the envelopes. Easy enough to make up a new — very simple — riddle and put it in your envelope.

'Pierre's grandson was looking after Loki so I was free to go up to the first floor of the tower and wait. However, I was already regretting the idea.'

'Not enough to stop you pushing me

217

down the stairs.'

He looked up, couldn't hold her gaze, looked away.

'No.'

'What about the amplifier?'

'Amplifier?'

'The one that gave me an electric shock. Just before the fashion show. You carried it into the grand salon. Did you tamper with it first?'

He shook his head.

'No. No, I . . . No!'

He appeared genuinely perplexed. But Grace recalled the amplifier's loose plug and Kai's insistence that he kept his equipment in excellent condition. Could Vespasien's protestations be nothing more than a clever act?

She sucked in a shaky breath.

'The deal with this business acquaintance of Johnno's — you realise it can't go ahead now. You'll have to cancel it.'

His head jerked back. He was looking at her as if she were mad.

'Why on earth should I do that, mademoiselle?' he asked with a full return to arrogance, and Grace was seized by the conviction that he might now regret his ill-judged attempt on her life, but certainly didn't regret selling his wine as something it was not.

'Have you any idea,' he went on, 'how much it costs to maintain and run this place? A small fortune, I assure you. Not to mention my dear wife who has great difficulty reining in her extravagances.'

Grace thought of Angela's beautiful but very expensive clothes and her lavish entertainments.

'What you're doing is fraud,' she persisted. 'Dishonest. There are other ways to make money.'

'Unfortunately, mademoiselle, the dishonest ways are often the most lucrative.'

The sound of footsteps on tiles broke the silence that fell. Kai came round the corner, two trailing cashmere scarves, one orange, one purple, draped over his arm. He'd plainly had trouble deciding.

'What's going on?' Frowning, he

looked from Grace to his stepfather. He stopped by the dining-room door, heard Loki scrabbling at the wood, and opened it.

The dog bounded up to his master in a flurry of legs and wagging tail. Vespasien crouched to fondle the setter's long silky ears.

'I'm a proud man,' he said with a glance at Kai who was heading towards the two of them. He spoke so quietly Grace knew only she was supposed to hear.

'I've always refused to allow my stepson to help me financially. I've never wanted, or asked for, his charity.' He straightened, pulling himself to full height. His eyes held hers. 'I'm in your hands, mademoiselle. Do your worst.'

With that he turned, passing Kai without a word before re-entering the dining room.

'Are you all right?' Grace could hear the concern in Kai's voice, saw it in his eyes.

She turned away, hugging her arms

across her chest. Her confrontation with Vespasien had shaken her. Conflicting emotions — anger, but pity too — swirled in her brain.

'I'm fine,' she said, eyes filling with tears.

'What were the two of you talking about?'

'Not now, Kai. Please.' She needed time to think, time to make sense of it all.

She jumped when his hands closed round her upper arms. He was behind her, and his lips brushed like a caress against her hair as he spoke.

'Are you sure you're all right?'

A single tear spilled over. She could feel it sliding down her cheek. She brought her hand up to cover his, but let it drop back to her side.

'I'll tell you tomorrow,' she said. She paused. 'Before I leave.'

A moment of stillness. Then Kai was turning her round, enfolding her in the warm strength of his arms, pressing her head against his shoulder.

'No. Tell me now.'

There was no avoiding it. Briefly, Grace closed her eyes and sucked in a long breath.

'Your stepfather's been relabelling rubbish wine and selling it as 2005 vintage.'

Kai stiffened.

'And for that he was all set to kill you?' She heard disbelief in the question, vying with anger.

'There's a lot of money involved.' Grace's voice was thick, reluctant. She'd never felt so wretched.

'Tell me. Tell me everything,' he urged. 'Start at the beginning.'

With a shaky intake of breath she did so, starting with the guided tour of the wine cellars and finishing with her confrontation with Vespasien. And all the while she spoke, Kai held her in his arms, stroking her hair, murmuring soft words of comfort and reassurance, and she wished her time with him didn't have to end.

At last she fell silent.

'I'm going to have to phone the gendarmes,' Kai said.

'I know.' First his brother, then his mother, now his stepfather — she was tearing Kai's family apart. The sooner she left the better.

She lifted her head from his shoulder and he drew away, hand going to his pocket for his phone.

'Kai, wait. Phone them later. Vespasien's secret is out.' She spoke quickly, anxious to convince. 'It's not just between him and me any more. He knows I'll have told you, which means he's no longer a threat to me. So phone the gendarmes later, after the meal. Let's all eat together, family and friends, one last time.'

'You think I can sit at the same table and calmly eat, knowing what my stepfather tried to do to you?'

'Maybe not.' Grace's voice was husky with emotion. She could see the pain and anger in his eyes, and the sight brought her own tears closer to the surface. 'But try — for your mother's sake.'

Was she doing the right thing? She didn't know. She only knew she couldn't face the thought of bringing yet more disruption to Kai's family.

And so they re-entered the dining-room and took their places, and she watched Kai smile and chat, eat something from every dish and taste every wine. Only the set line of his jaw and the narrowing of his eyes each time he looked at his stepfather told her the effort it cost him. And if Vespasien was wondering what was going on, well, let him wonder.

Grace too played her part, and hoped no-one would guess that she was crying inside, beset by a grief that swelled and twisted without end.

★ ★ ★

The following morning before breakfast, Grace let herself through the low door and on to the circular platform that formed the roof of the tower. She stood looking out, forearms resting on the chest-high wall.

It was very still, with not a breath of movement in the freezing cold air. Dawn was breaking, a pearly grey glow in the east while further to the west, where the sky shaded to indigo, one of the planets — Venus, she thought — shone brightly close to the horizon.

Snow-covered hills, crossed by lines of trees and stone walls, stretched out in front and to her left, while to her right stood the dark snow-capped trees of the forest she and Natasha had driven through on their arrival.

How much had happened since then. And now it was over. One of Pierre's cousins would soon be clearing the road of snow, the gendarmes were coming at nine to take statements — and to take Vespasien away? — then she and Natasha would leave, heading for the ferry port and the UK.

It was Christmas Day but she couldn't rejoice. She felt empty, drained of all emotion.

Perhaps the soft click of the door latch had alerted her, she didn't know, but she wasn't surprised when Kai joined her. Deep in her heart, she'd known he'd come here.

In so many ways they were on the same wavelength. In other circumstances . . .

She bit her lip and tried to banish the thought. A lasting relationship between the two of them was unthinkable, impossible — even more so after all that had happened.

Knowing it, though, didn't make it any easier to face the truth of it.

Kai stood behind her, his arms crisscrossing round her neck, a welcome weight on her shoulders. His chin rested lightly on the top of her head.

'I don't want you to go,' he said.

'I have to.' Tears had filled her eyes, and she was glad he couldn't see her face. 'I've caused enough damage round here already. And . . .'

'And what?' he prompted when her voice caught.

'There's no future for the two of us, Kai.'

'Don't say that.' And all at once he was

twisting her round to face him. One hand was at her waist, pulling her against him, the other at her nape, tangling in her hair, and she gasped as his lips claimed hers in a kiss that sent fierce desire shooting through her. 'I love you, Grace. Together, we can make a future — our future. We can make it happen.'

How tempting it would be! How tempting to yield to the beauty of his kiss, his sweet words. But she mustn't do it. Too much had come between them. It would never work.

'No, Kai,' she said softly, pulling away.

The sky was much lighter now. From afar came the rumble of a heavy vehicle moving slowly. The snow plough was doing its job. The day was getting underway.

But for Grace it felt as if the day was already over.

New Beginning

Four days.

Grace moved restlessly between the lounge and kitchen of the house on the coast she rented with three friends. She had the place to herself. It was late on New Year's Eve, and the others were out partying.

They'd been the happiest four days of her life. The danger she'd faced had faded to a distant, unreal memory — while the love she'd shared with Kai remained frighteningly vivid.

A week had gone by and she couldn't stop thinking about him, couldn't rid her mind of the memories — the warmth of his hand round hers, the strength of his arms as they enfolded her, the fierce intensity of his kisses and, too, that ease in each other's company, that precious sense of togetherness.

Fighting back the tears, she touched her fingers to the sketch in its gilded frame that sat on the mantelpiece propped against the wall. It was one of Cameron's clever pen-and-ink drawings, and her thoughts flashed back to the day he'd given it to her.

Christmas Day, the fifth day of their stay at the Château Beauvallon, and definitely not a happy one. The memory of it numbed her still.

The faces stood out above all. Angela's, brittle and weighed down by guilt. Barbs's, sad and soft with concern. Even Johnno had looked subdued. And all of them had been trying to keep up a pretence of normality even though everyone now knew Vespasien had pushed Grace down the tower steps and why he'd done it.

The gendarmes had taken her statement in the dining-room. Kai had sat on the other side of the table — as far away from her as possible? — ready to translate if necessary. His expression was set in grim, taut lines.

She longed to reach across the table, take his hand in hers, give it a comforting squeeze. But the distance between them had seemed unbridgeable and her hands had stayed in her lap.

Another face, Vespasien's, an aristocratic mask revealing nothing as he left his home, a gendarme on either side.

'Natasha and I will be leaving very shortly,' Grace had said to Kai. They stood in the vast entrance hall watching his stepfather's departure.

Angela was a few metres away, crying quietly into a handkerchief. Barbs had put her arms round her and was patting her back and making soothing noises.

Cameron and Natasha were standing close together. He'd taken her hands in his, while Johnno, looking uncomfortable, was pulling his cigarettes and lighter out of his pocket.

'There's no need to see us off,' Grace had continued. Though neither of them had moved, the distance between them seemed to have grown greater still.

'As you wish.' Kai's eyes met hers. The expression on his face was unreadable, his tone was devoid of emotion, but she thought she could see pain in his eyes, and it tore at her heart.

She'd felt her face crumpling.

'I must finish packing,' she'd man-aged, blinking furiously to hold back the tears as she twisted away, heading for the stairs.

She could hear the sound of her own breathing loud in her ears, and the clack of Natasha's high heels on marble as she followed her. But it was Angela's quiet sobs that echoed over and over in her mind.

It was all Grace's fault. She was the one who had ripped this family apart. She alone was responsible. How could she ever forgive herself?

When the two sisters came downstairs a quarter of an hour later, they'd found Cameron waiting for them by the Christmas tree.

'This is for you, Natasha.' With the side of his boot, he slid a heavy package wrapped in shiny gold paper a few inches forward. 'I'll carry it to your car for you. It's your present from all of us. My step-father chose it. A case of Château

Beauvallon bubbly. Don't worry, it's genuine. Hey, sorry, bad taste,' he added with a laugh.

He bent to pick up a smaller package from the foot of the tree.

'And this is for you, Grace. My choice for you. Happy Christmas.'

Bringing herself back to the present, Grace now ran her fingers round the frame. The sketch showed her face in semi-profile. She was smiling. There was a radiance about her in the portrait. Cameron had captured it perfectly. And it was a bittersweet sorrow to see it, for it was the radiance of a woman in love.

★ ★ ★

The doorbell rang. Grace looked at her phone and frowned. It had gone 11. She wasn't expecting anyone.

She'd arranged to have lunch with her parents and Natasha the next day, so it was unlikely to be them. Friends, maybe, wondering why she'd been avoiding them

232

all since returning from France, insisting she see the New Year in? Or friends of one of her housemates?

It was Kai on the doorstep, a tall shadowy figure in the light that spilled out from the hall, and her heart did a crazy somersault. Her face, her whole being, lit up. She couldn't help it. Pleasure at seeing him was like a warm glow speeding through her like wildfire.

For the space of a heartbeat, his face too lit up, she was sure of it. Then cold air gusted in through the open door. She took in the set of his face, now stark and unsmiling, and shivered.

She'd been mistaken. Nothing had changed, and it was as if something inside her froze. Her smile faltered before sliding from her face.

'Kai. Do you want to come in? How did you know where I lived?' The words came in a rush.

'Angela gave me your sister's e-mail address,' he said, stepping into the hallway. 'She told me.'

And Natasha had said nothing! Grace

thought. She could at least have warned her.

'Come on in. Let me take your coat. Sit down.' Conscious she was babbling, Grace forced herself to take a long, steadying breath. 'What can I get you to drink?'

'Nothing, thanks. I won't keep you long. I want to bring you up to speed with what's been happening, that's all.'

Both his expression and tone were neutral. He was a polite stranger. Nothing more. He unbuttoned his long wool coat but kept it on, and remained standing in the centre of the lounge, looking round.

'I share with three others,' she said, feeling the need to explain the marvellous mix of colours and styles in the objects displayed on the walls and shelves. She, too, stayed standing, and couldn't help inhaling the smoky notes of his cologne.

'I remember. You told me.' He paused, and Grace had the impression his thoughts had slipped back to the previous week. 'Barbs and Johnno left the same day you did.' He sighed. 'There won't be any more business deals — of any kind — with Johnno in the future.' An edge of steel had entered his voice, and Grace was in no doubt Kai had been the one who'd laid down the new ground rules.

'Cameron has promised me,' he went on, 'that he'll never copy a Sisley or any other painting ever again. He'll concentrate on his own work from now on. He's going to Paris tomorrow to join his lover. A fresh start for him.'

'His New Year's resolution,' Grace said, and a smile came unbidden to her face as she remembered. Cameron had spoken about making big changes in his life. 'I hope he'll be very happy.'

'Yes, so do I.'

Their eyes met in a brief instant of fellow-feeling before he looked elsewhere.

'My mother has also made a promise.' There was pain as well as steel in Kai's voice now. 'If she decides to sell something that doesn't belong to her, she will at least ask the owner's permission first.'

He fell silent, and Grace was all too wretchedly aware of the pain and disruption she'd caused. Kai's family would never be the same again — and it was all her fault.

'And Vespasien?' Her voice had dropped to little more than a whisper.

'He's been allowed back home for the time being. He'll be charged with attempted murder and fraud. There's a possibility he'll be acquitted on the attempted murder charge because you weren't sure he actually intended to kill you — and he denies it. If found guilty, he could get anything up to five years in jail.'

Grace sucked in a shaky breath.

'I hope he is acquitted, Kai. He's not a bad man at heart.' Another silence, broken when Kai crossed to the mantelpiece and picked up Cameron's sketch of Grace. For a fraction of a second he simply looked at the drawing. Grace couldn't tell from his expression what he was thinking.

'We have to talk,' he said, replacing

the sketch. 'Put your coat on. We'll walk down to the beach.'

'We've said all that needs to be said.' What on earth could they have to talk about? It was over between them.

'I disagree.'

And Grace gave in, the thought of a short time more in Kai's company bringing an ache that was both pleasure and pain to her heart.

The wind off the sea was cold and moist with the tang of salt. She pulled the collar of her padded jacket up round her ears and recalled with a pang the still air of Kai's part of France.

They walked side by side, not touching, along the 100 or so metres to the end of Grace's road. It wasn't until they crossed the main road and were on the beach that Kai started to speak.

'You said, that last morning, on the roof of the tower, you said you blamed yourself for tearing my family apart.'

'That's right.' Grace's feet crunched across the pebbles that shifted and slid beneath her. She was glad the light from

237

the streetlamps high above the main road barely reached the shingle. She didn't want Kai to see her face. The crash of wind-driven waves was loud in her ears.

'But you're wrong,' he said. 'It's hardly your fault. You didn't make my brother forge a major artwork. You didn't force my mother to make money by selling one of her husband's paintings. And it was entirely my stepfather's choice to pass a mediocre vintage off as an excellent one.'

'I was the catalyst,' Grace said unhappily. 'If I hadn't been there . . .'

'No.' Abruptly he stopped and turned, facing her. He closed his hands round her upper arms so that she lifted troubled eyes to his. 'In their various ways they were doing wrong. They'd have been found out sooner or later. You being there made it happen sooner, maybe — and that's a good thing, surely.'

Grace looked away, beyond him to the wide sweep of the bay. Lights glittered and sparkled all along its length. Overhead, a crowd of gulls screamed and shrieked as they flew inland.

What he was saying made sense, she thought, and the notion ignited a tiny spark of hope deep inside her.

'I thought you blamed me. You were so cold and angry.'

'Angry with them. I love my mother and brother dearly. Up till now I've always respected Vespasien. But there were times when I was ashamed of the three of them, and that made me angry — with myself. Can you understand that? My family had shown themselves to be a bunch of crooks. My stepfather had tried to kill you. How could I possibly ask you to . . .'

'Ask me what, Kai?' The breath had caught in her throat.

'You love me, Grace. I know you do. Cameron saw it, too. It shines out of that sketch he did.'

His tone had softened, grown huskier, and he drew her closer. Though the light was poor, she sensed something very loving about the look he gave her as he smoothed strands of her hair back from her face.

'We haven't known each other long, Grace. But sometimes you know, straight away, that you've met the person you can't bear to live without. That's how I feel about you.'

He gathered her closer still, hands going to her back, pulling her to him.

'I'm asking you to marry me, Grace. Will you be my wife?'

She didn't hesitate.

'Yes, Kai, I will.'

And all along the coast, fireworks cracked and popped into life, signalling midnight, the new year, and a wonderful new beginning.